# WORLD WAR III

D0528951

# WORLD WAR III

A novelisation by Brian Harris

Based upon the original
screenplay by Robert L. Joseph

NEW ENGLISH LIBRARY

First published in the USA in 1982 by Pocket Books, a Simon and Schuster division of Gulf & Western Corporation

First NEL Paperback Edition March 1982

NEL Books are published by
New English Library,
Mill Road, Dunton Green,
Sevenoaks, Kent,
a division of Hodder & Stoughton Ltd.

Made and printed in Great Britain by
Cox & Wyman Ltd, Reading

**Harris, Brian**

World War III.
I. Title II. Joseph, Robert L.
813'.54[F]   PS3569.A/

ISBN 0-450-05488-8

# PART ONE

Silent. Awesome. Majestic. Everlastingly beautiful. Untouched by history. That was the description a Russian Orthodox missionary noted in his personal journal in 1794 as his impression of this section of rock and snow of what later came to be called the Brooks Range inside the Arctic Circle of Alaska's northernmost province. They are the first-known words written about the North Slope.

What he might have written, if he'd had the chance, was that it was also unforgiving.

The missionary's frozen body—his journal and Bible clutched together in one hand—was discovered in 1974 by a pipeline worker who'd chipped off a piece of the Russian's knee with a pickax before he realized he wasn't just hacking at subzero ground.

In the 160 years that the missionary rested undisturbed and surrounded by silent beauty little had changed. The Brooks Range remains for the most part unexplored and unsettled. It has been defaced infrequently by pockets of civilization, inhabited by foolish or brave souls whose very survival depends upon winning a constant battle against nature and the delivery of supplies from other souls even more foolish or brave.

The Russian Christian's impression of awesome majesty, particularly his appreciation of everlasting beauty, is unchallengeable and will continue to be until there is no one left to record it. However, his sense of history or rather his view of geopolitics, if indeed he had one, would certainly be obsolete today. The world politics of nations has substantially changed since Catherine Romanov reigned as empress of the Russian Empire, and George Washington began his second term as president, struggling with the internal affairs of a new and arrogant republic and advocating no permanent foreign alliances. That their two nations would one day face each other as wary antagonists across a frozen expanse of incredible beauty is no less ironic than, some predicted, inevitable.

USAF T/Sgt. Willard J. Stedman was not concerned with the consequences of geopolitical theory, inevitable or otherwise. His preoccupation with sleep, that is, longing for it, kept him awake. That, and the half dozen radar and weather-satellite screens at the console before him. Stedman stared at the computer-defined translation of the latest weather-satellite photo. The screen was a mass of electronic colors representing identifiable terrain features of the Chartosk Peninsula of the Soviet Arctic to the north, across the Bering Strait to the Seward Peninsula to the west and the Brooks Range and Philip Smith Mountains to the east. The image was laced with grid coordinates and alphanumeric data, all of which meant that the storm that raged outside the relative comfort of this Quonset hut would continue for at least several more days. It didn't bother him that there was a storm—he wasn't going anywhere—but his personal supply of peach preserves was nearly exhausted. T/Sgt. Stedman had a thing about peach preserves. He craved peach preserves the way others chain-smoked. He ate peach preserves on nearly anything that was edible and some things that weren't. When there wasn't anything to put it on he just ate it with a spoon out of the jar. He *loved* peach preserves. His mother made them back home in Arkansas and she sent him a carefully packed carton of two dozen jars once a month. That was the trouble. The supply chopper was late this week and if this storm delayed it another couple of days—which seemed increasingly probable—then he'd run out of peach preserves.

Stedman spread a glob of preserves on a cracker and munched as he considered one of the radar screens. A man shouldn't have to be deprived of something as simple as his preserves, he told himself. You'd think the United States Air Force would be sympathetic to a guy up here, especially in a place like this. Dewline Radar Station #68. It was so far out of reach they couldn't even think of a decent name for it. Six men in two Quonset huts for four months at a time. It wasn't that he was a complainer, but—goddamnit!—what was he going to do when he ran out?

Lt. Bradford Kennedy closed the shaving kit and tucked it under his arm. He'd been up since midnight. He hadn't slept well in the last two days since he'd heard from Fairbanks. They'd told him bad weather was coming and to be on the alert, Dewline #68 was a crucially important outpost. It was nice to hear that someone appreciated him inasmuch as superiors didn't usually have much to say regarding job performance unless you'd screwed up. Not that he was a screw-up; no one got to be a first lieutenant in the United States Air Force, assigned to Dewline primary radar of NORAD's Alaskan Defense Command, by making mistakes. Not with his job.

Kennedy left his office and walked down the narrow corridor to the ops room. T/Sgt. Stedman had the graveyard shift this morning. That was fortunate and unfortunate, Kennedy thought. Stedman was very good, very reliable. But he ate that damned jelly and everything he touched got sticky.

"How's it going, Stedman?" Kennedy moved to the coffee machine. He set his shaving kit down and drew a cup of coffee.

"Hey, Lieutenant." Stedman turned, shrugged with a smile. "Usual. The satellite shows the front building over Chartosk. Otherwise, quiet."

"Coffee?"

"Yes, sir. Please. Black."

Kennedy drew another cup. He crossed to the console and set it beside the tech sergeant.

"Thank you, sir. You're up early, Lieutenant."

Kennedy nodded. "Couldn't sleep." He moved to the duty desk and glanced through the message log. Through a partially open door he heard snoring and walked to it to peer inside.

"Wilkinson," Stedman said. "Never knew a guy could make so much noise unconscious."

"Everyone down?"

"Till six."

"Who's relief?"

"Myerson."

Kennedy nodded again, satisfied. He went back to the coffee machine for more sugar then sat at the duty desk. A week-old copy of *Newsweek* was stuffed in the top drawer. President Thomas McKenna faced Senator Milton Weston on the cover. Lightning bolts separated the two old rivals. Politics. The presidential sweepstakes was starting. Again. The first primaries would begin in less than three months, Kennedy realized without enthusiasm. He turned to the sports news.

It began with a blinking light. Kennedy had read all that interested him in the news magazine and had turned to the featured interview in *Playboy* when he heard Stedman's chair squeak suddenly. He looked up to see the alert light blinking on the long-range-tracking radar console.

"Lieutenant." Stedman's voice was calm but serious.

"What is it?"

"I have a blip. North quadrant, Tango-Charlie sector."

Kennedy got up from his place at the duty desk. He took his shaving kit and moved behind Stedman's chair. "What've we got?"

The tech sergeant adjusted the scope he was staring at. "I don't know."

"What range?"

"Ah, two hundred . . . no, one-seventy miles. At one thousand five. Speed . . ." He changed to another scope. "Two-seventy knots. It's a bird, all right." Stedman looked back at Kennedy. "Ahead of the front. Do we have anything up?"

Kennedy shook his head. "No."

Stedman was slightly shaken. He looked back at his screens. "Whoever it is, he's on the deck."

"How many?"

"Just one, Lieutenant. We're getting tracks from just one plane."

"You're sure?"

"Yes, sir." Stedman nervously licked at a sticky finger and punched up a computer display that printed out a mapped grid of coordinates centered around a bright red blip. Beside the blip was a flashing message, UNIDENTIFIED TARGET, with alphanumeric data on speed, direction, altitude and course. "It's air-breathing, all right. It's too slow and too low to be anything else."

Kennedy nodded. "You're right." He opened the shaving kit.

"I'd better notify Elmendorf," Stedman said quickly. He wasn't just serious or just excited anymore, Kennedy realized by the tone of his voice. He was frightened. "NORAD will have to be—"

"I don't think so," Kennedy replied calmly. He'd already screwed the silencer over the barrel of the automatic pistol as Stedman half-turned to face him.

"But, Lieu—"

The pistol barely moved in his hand as he pulled the

trigger. Kennedy had never used a silencer before, and the only immediate evidence that the weapon had fired was the quiet *phhumpt* from its muzzle and the maroonish-black hole the slug made in T/Sgt. Willard J. Stedman's forehead.

The NCO's head was snapped backward by the impact and his body immediately lost all coordination, slipping out of the chair, knocking over a half-filled jar of peach preserves from the console and falling to the floor with a hard thud. Kennedy stood over him a few seconds, the weapon trained on the base of the skull, but there was no movement.

Lieutenant Kennedy then went into the sleeping quarters and, standing over each of the occupied cots in turn, fired once into his sleeping victims. When he returned to the ops room, the snoring had ceased.

The blip on the screen was still blinking as he dragged Stedman's body a few feet away from the console and sat in the controller's chair. He stared at the screen as he made his call to Elmendorf.

"Hello, six-eight, what's up?" said a slightly bored voice on the line.

Kennedy checked his watch. It was exactly 0500 hours.

"Lieutenant Kennedy. We've got a bad generator here, throwing voltage fits. It's screwing up our high-band reception."

"So?"

"I'm requesting permission to shut down for a few minutes. We can fix it, but nobody wants to get near the damn thing while it's fritzing like this."

"Terrific."

Kennedy took a long breath. "Okay?"

"Wait a minute." There was a muffled conversation at the other end, then: "Kennedy, this is Colonel Clark. What's the matter up there?"

"Generator, sir. We're losing our number one. I can't switch to the reserve without blowing out the main. We need to shut down for a few minutes to make the crossover."

"Christ!"

"It won't take long, Colonel."

*"How* long?"

"Ten minutes. Fifteen at the outside."

"What's your LRS?"

Kennedy watched the numbers change beside the blip. The plane was already descending. In five minutes no one would ever have known it was there. "Clear, Colonel. Everything's clear here. Just like always."

"All right, do it. But check in as soon as you're up. Got that?"

"Yes, sir."

"If World War Three starts, I'm blaming you."

"Don't worry, sir," Lieutenant Kennedy said. "I'm in control here."

## BROOKS MOUNTAIN RANGE 0505 HRS
## 70 MILES NORTH DEWLINE STA. #68

Major Sergei Devenko tugged at his arctic gloves. He was seated on a snowmobile, and a few feet away a red flare burned brilliantly. He adjusted his goggles and scanned the sky again with binoculars. He could hear the sound of the plane but couldn't see it yet. The binoculars were nearly useless in tracking the sound because it seemed to be everywhere—the icy tundra had that effect. Sound waves bounced crazily in this frigid stillness, but he used them anyway, searching the compass heading that would bring in the last plane.

Devenko never saw the aircraft. Instead, he saw the billowing parachutes. A few at first, then dozens, until the sky was littered with them. He tossed out another flare and started the snowmobile.

They were landing all around him and he shouted hoarse instructions as he maneuvered the machine across the tundra. They were dressed in identical white arctic gear—parkas, boots, gloves, helmets—and cinched tightly across their chests were webbed nylon belts that secured automatic weapons to their backs. A single red star on their helmets, emblem of the Soviet Army, was the only identifiable marking visible on their gear. They hit the snow wordlessly, quickly burying their parachutes and moving out toward the glow of the flares. It was the proudest moment in Major Devenko's career. These were the elite. The most dedicated, the best-trained and best-equipped fighting troops of the most powerful army in the world—the 9th Soviet Division, 51st Arctic Combat Brigade. So far the mission had been flawless. Nothing had gone wrong. Nothing *would* go wrong, Devenko was confident. They'd planned too long for this operation.

"Stop that yelling!"

Devenko swerved to avoid a paratrooper who'd just landed and rolled to his feet. The major recognized him immediately. His parka hood was light blue to distinguish it from the others. He was Col. Alexander Vorashin, brigade commander and commander of this special strike force. The leaders' leader, as far as the major was concerned.

"Welcome to Alaska, Colonel," Devenko said in a loud whisper. He dismounted from the snowmobile as Vorashin quickly gathered his parachute. "It is a beautiful sight, all our—"

Vorashin silenced him with a look. "Your voice echoes like a howitzer here, Sergei," the colonel said with quiet menace. "Shut up."

Devenko bowed his head, nodded. "I'm sorry, Alex. The excitement—"

Vorashin nodded impatiently. "Of course." A muscle twitched at the back of his jaw. "Please tell me about the vehicles, Sergei. We are wasting time standing here."

Vorashin had been a friend for nearly twenty years. Devenko had never known him when he wasn't in a hurry. His specialty had been American tactics. Perhaps that explained it. "Undamaged," the major said. "All troop and armament vehicles landed without damage. Two snowmobiles, however, refuse to start."

"Bury them." Vorashin glanced over his shoulder as two soldiers landed together a few meters away. He looked back to Devenko. "We don't leave anything behind."

"Yes, I'll see to it."

Another paratrooper in a light green hood approached and Vorashin hand-signaled for him to move toward the flare. The colonel swore to himself as the man passed. Devenko squinted after the soldier. He didn't recognize him. He was wearing the green hood reserved for communications officers, but the major didn't recognize him. Devenko knew all the officers and most of the men. He turned quickly to Vorashin.

"Who—"

"A last-minute recruit," the colonel said bitterly. "Nicolai Saamaretz. *Major* Nicolai Saamaretz."

Devenko frowned. "I don't understand, Alex. What—"

"He is Rudenski's spy. He is along to watch and report."

"Rudenski? What has the KGB to do with—"

"*This* is a KGB operation," Vorashin said quietly. His eyes flashed anger.

Devenko didn't understand immediately. "No one told me—" He stopped when the colonel gave him a grim look.

"Apparently it wasn't necessary for us to know before," Vorashin replied.

"But Colonel, General Rudenski isn't our commander in chief!" Devenko cried.

"*He* is giving the orders, Sergei," Vorashin said. "And *we* follow orders. End of discussion."

The Soviet major nodded. "Yes, my Colonel. Anyway, the KGB is not our enemy."

"The Americans are not our enemies either," Vorashin said quickly. "Remember that, Sergei. Remember that well."

"And this mission?"

"A tactical defense. Just as you were briefed. The operation's objective has not changed." Vorashin turned briskly toward the glow of the dying flares as if to direct his anger elsewhere. "Come along, Sergei. We aren't invited guests here. There is much to do and little time to get it done."

"The clock ticks?" It was a favorite expression of Col. Alexander Vorashin's. It meant "move your ass." Major Devenko noticed the slightest hint of a smile cross his commander's lips.

"Yes, Major, the clock ticks."

The officers'-club party room was crowded, noisy and polluted with cigarette smoke. The cocktail party was only thirty minutes old and Lt. Col. Jacob Caffey was already wishing the enormous Christmas tree in the center of the room would catch fire or someone's wife would faint or the booze would suddenly run out. He wished anything would happen that would allow him to escape this silly madness.

There were a hundred kinds of duty Jake Caffey despised. High on the list was attending "official" parties. He didn't like to get dressed for them because wearing his dress uniform—besides being uncomfortable and sweaty—made him feel like a jumped-up mannequin. He didn't like parties because most of the people who attended them were either idiots, or bores, or their spouses, which meant the same thing. He didn't like the stifling air, or the smoke, or the jokes (they were always the same; old, bad and stupid or new, bad and stupid). He had difficulty remembering names, which was bad politically even if he didn't care who was

who or that the lush with halitosis trying to seduce any
D-cup present was aide to a congressman on the
military appropriations committee.

But mostly, Colonel Caffey hated this party particularly because he was guest of honor and he *couldn't* get
out of it. It was his "send-off" party. In a few hours (he
kept checking his watch for reassurance) he'd be leaving Bragg. It was a bittersweet transfer. He loved the
82nd Airborne Infantry as much as an officer could love
a unit—he'd been in it since graduation from West
Point, nearly eleven years—and he'd miss it, despite
the occasional parties. He was going north, to a
new and challenging assignment. But Nancy couldn't
come, at least not right away, and that bothered him.
It wasn't the best time for picking up and moving
out. His marriage was not exactly the strong bond
it appeared to be. Nancy was just about at the end of
her rope with the unrelenting schedule he'd put himself through these last several months. There was a
brief respite of joy when he'd told her that he'd,
reluctantly, put in for transfer. Nancy beamed trium-
phantly for weeks until he got his orders to his new
duty station. Fairbanks, Alaska, in the middle of winter, was not the ideal place to start rebuilding a marriage.

"Everybody? Everybody, quiet a minute. Listen
up." A burly major with a crew cut climbed on a chair
and raised his glass. "Everybody, fill your glasses."

Caffey shook his head. "Christ," he said to himself.
Nancy tugged at his sleeve. She was easily the most
beautiful woman at this disaster. That was part of the
trouble. Her beauty disguised a shrewish, ambitious
woman whose concern for her husband's career masked
a burning desire to reach a higher social level. Nancy
Caffey was meant to be a general's wife. That Caffey
wasn't was *his* fault.

"Jake, for godsakes stand up straight. Major Timmons is going to make a toast."

"I don't want to be toasted," Caffey said quietly to
her.

"He's a bright young man, Gene Timmons." She smiled and raised her glass in answer to the major's gesture.

"He's drunk," Caffey said.

"Will you *please* try not to look as if this were a lynching. This party is in your honor."

"Well, you know what I think of—"

"This is to the best G-3 training and operations officer in the entire 82nd Airborne, if not the entire US Army," Timmons began, swaying slightly on his chair. "A fighting leader whose attributes include the patience and compassion of George Patton, the tactical genius of George Marshall and the dedication to duty of George Armstrong Custer. To the youngest light colonel in the division with a jump on becoming its youngest brigadier . . ."

"This is ridiculous," Caffey whispered.

"Shut up, darling."

". . . we wish all the best and good luck to Lieutenant Colonel 'Big Jake' Caffey. Give 'em hell in the Yukon, sir." Major Timmons drained his glass. There was a hush in the room as glasses were tilted upward in unison.

"I'll second that."

Caffey glanced quickly to the entrance as Brigadier General Walter Selby sauntered in smiling.

"Oh, God," Caffey muttered to himself.

"I hope you don't mind my crashing your little party, Jake," the general said as he crossed to Caffey. They shook hands. "I couldn't resist."

"Walt . . . I mean, General. I'm embarrassed for all—"

"Hell, don't apologize. I'll tell you what. If they were sending *me* to Alaska, you can be goddamn sure I'd have a bash to mark the occasion." The general nodded politely to Nancy. "How do, Nance. We're going to miss this oaf, you know."

She smiled politely but without affection. "I'm sure you will, General." In her next breath, thinly disguising her effort to get away, she turned to Caffey. "Excuse me, darling, but I have to check on the punch. Shall I get you some?"

"No, thanks. General?"

"No, I'm not much for punch at these things. That's usually what it is."

Nancy squeezed Caffey's hand. "Don't forget to circulate. This *is* for you, remember."

When she was gone Selby said, "Still blames me for your transfer to Outer Mongolia, eh, Jake?"

"She knows better, General."

"And you can drop that 'General' crap. I didn't come here just because you're a damned good officer that I don't like losing. Generals, contrary to popular belief, do have friends in the ranks."

Caffey smiled genuinely for the first time since he'd arrived. "Thanks, Walt. This wasn't my idea, I guess I don't have to tell you."

"Jake Caffey at a full-dress party? Why do you think I showed up? That *is* you under all that spit and polish?"

"Nancy was so insistent—"

"Say no more. I shudder to think what grand scheme Edna would come up with." The general paused to look around. "Speaking of grandness, where is Diana, the real glory of the Caffey household?"

"It's exam time."

"They take exams in the seventh grade?"

"I don't know, but they do in the ninth grade."

"Jesus, where'd I lose two years?"

Caffey shrugged. "Same place I did. Last month I said she was twelve. She's thirteen. She cried for an hour. Teenagers are very sensitive about that sort of thing."

"The little princess."

"That's out these days, too. She'd prefer to be called Diane or Diana Elizabeth. Deedee is out. So is Blonde Beauty and Twinkletoes. I'm Father; Nancy is Mother, but Richard K. Fredricks, Jr., the tenth-grade quarterback with pimples for brains, is Dickie. You figure it out."

Selby laughed. "You are entering the age of love, Jake. It starts now and doesn't ever stop."

"You're a big help."

"Wait until she hits sixteen. You think the Alaskan Defense Command will be trying? Just wait three years. You don't know the terror a grown man can suffer from a one-hundred-pound sixteen-year-old daughter."

"Horror stories I don't need tonight."

Nancy was weaving through the crowd back toward them when Selby saw her. He gripped Caffey by the shoulder. "I'd better vamoose before she bites off my other leg, Jake. You know I don't like seeing you leave this outfit of screw-ups. When you get tired of igloos and Eskimo Pie, just give me a call."

"Sure."

"I mean it, Jake. Anything you need up there, you let me know. Gard Roberts can be a pissant."

"I'll remember, Walt. Thanks."

As Nancy approached, Selby said, "Just leaving, pretty lady. As becomes my rank, character and influence, I shall engage in some serious drinking with the ever-ready warriors of the infamous 82nd." He winked at her and moved toward a group near the Christmas tree.

She handed Caffey a small glass of punch. "Here, you need to hold something. You look like a bored doorman the way you stand with your hands behind your back."

"I *feel* like a doorman. Look, let's slip out of here—"

"Not *now*. You haven't met some of these people. There's a Mr. Whorley from Congressman Gilbert's staff and—"

"I *met* Whorley," Caffey said with a strained smile. "I've been watching him watching you. The little prick's spilled his drink twice trying to get a better look at your cleavage. Not that he has to try very hard. Did you have to wear *that* dress?"

"I don't have my Eskimo sealskins yet, darling," she

said viciously. "What was so amusing with the general, if I might ask? Something about me?"

"We were talking about kids. Deedee, as a matter of fact."

"Did you remember her?"

Caffey let out a sigh. "Nancy, please."

"I don't know how he ever got to be a general. He doesn't act like one."

"Walt Selby is the finest—"

"Yes, of course, dear," she said, nodding impatiently. "Now, there's someone I want you to meet." Nancy raised up on her tiptoes to see. "Yes, there they are. Bill and Mary Tretton. They have a son at Harvard. Bill's a major contributor to—"

"I'm leaving," Caffey cut in. He drained his glass of punch. "My feet hurt and my shirt is soaking wet."

"Jake, you can't leave!"

"Watch."

"If you think—"

Caffey turned to her. With quiet menace he said, "What I think is this, Nancy. I'm tired. I want to get out of these clothes and spend some time with our daughter before I have to leave this place. You stay here. You're better at this than I am. It's what you live for, anyway. So you just entertain until the punch gives out. I'll be at home."

"Goddamn you," she said in a low breath.

"Yes, I love you too, dear." He handed her the empty punch glass. "My flight leaves at 0130. I hope I see you before I go. I would kind of like one of those old-fashioned airport send-offs. You know, wife kisses husband with tear in her eye as he marches off to duty. I know it's utter melodrama and shamelessly sexist, but what the hell . . . I'm a sonofabitch like George Patton, a workaholic like George Marshall and an egomaniac like George Custer. What can you expect?" Then he kissed her lightly on the cheek and left.

## JONES'S STRIP
## NORTH SLOPE 0830 HRS

Remnants of a wind sock flapped violently as snow flurries whipped across the small runway. In the distance, above two abandoned metal hangars, the outline of Mt. Doonerak was barely visible through the haze. At the near end of the runway smoke escaped in swirling gusts from the chimney of a tiny log cabin attached to a Quonset hut. The only other sign of life was a Husky pawing for better refuge against the wind beneath the skeletal remains of a Cessna tail section.

The Pathfinder patrol leader gave a quick hand signal. Several meters away, what appeared to be a lump of snow moved. Then another. They made no sound in the lash of wind.

Arnold Jones adjusted the squelch on the shortwave set, making a face as a piercing bit of static blasted from the speaker. He was sitting before what his wife called his "radio things," though more accurately they were a considerable investment in high- and low-band-frequency radio transceivers. Jones had been a ham operator for more than thirty-five years. He'd developed lasting friendships with people he'd never met from Cape Town to Perth. He'd spoken to Albert Schweitzer at his Lambarene hospital in 1948 and to Dr. V. E. Fuchs at the South Pole on his historic first land-crossing of Antarctica in 1958. He'd talked to folks tens of thousands of miles away, but at the moment he was having trouble getting the powerful station at Fairbanks just 260 miles south of his little strip.

The voice Jones had lost finally returned but it was still weak, competing through storm-inspired static with severe high-band twang. "Fairbanks to Poppa seven-niner-zero. Fairbanks to— . . . ven-niner-zero. You still— . . . oppa?"

"Hel-lo, Fair-banks," he said with exaggerated enunciation. "You-are-weak-and-break-king-up. How-do-you-read? Over."

"Same-same," came the fading voice. "Better— . . . this fast. What is your sit— . . . tion? Over."

Jones noted the wind gauge mounted on the wall over the radio. "Reading eighteen knots from the southwest. Gusts to twenty-five. Looks like a dandy on the way. Over."

He stared at the speaker several moments waiting for a response. The interference was heavy enough to cut with a knife.

"Say again direc— . . . please."

Jones held the microphone closer to his lips. "South-west-at-one-eight. Again. South-west-at-eight-teen. One-eight-knots. Over."

Martha Jones walked sleepily from the bedroom. She went to her husband, yawned, folded the top of her flannel robe together and kissed him on the forehead. She was sixty-four yesterday and they'd celebrated the event last night in bed after a dinner of turkey and beans and red wine from California. Just like they'd done every year since she was twenty-two.

Martha settled into a nearby chair. "Fairbanks?"
Jones nodded.

"I copy." The radio voice crackled. "One-eigh—ots.
You folks— . . . kay? Over."

"Fine, thanks." Arnold winked at his wife. "Over."

"Tell them what a sexy old goat you are, Arnold
William Jones," Martha teased.

"I'm the one should still be in bed," he whispered.

"Better throw another log on the fire, folks," the
voice announced in a sudden burst of clarity. "Better
batten down up there. We've got a low-pressure front
moving north through the Aleutians. Most—" The rest
was drowned out as the interference reasserted itself.

"Young fella thinks we never saw a blow before,
mother," Jones said. He flipped on his microphone. "I-
read-you-Fairbanks. Thanks-for-the-warning. Poppa-
down. Seven-niner-zero-out."

Jones set the mike back in its place and switched off
the sets. "Well, that's it until Thursday."

Martha walked to the kitchen side of the cabin.
"Hungry?"

"Like a bear." He rubbed his back. "Sore, too."

"You're an old man." She started water in the sink.
"Pancakes or eggs?"

"Both, I think. Suppose I could shave before breakfast?"

"Ten minutes, then I start without you."

He got up from his chair and was nearly to the
bedroom when the Husky suddenly started barking.
Jones stopped at a window, rubbed a circle in the foggy
glass. "Damn."

"What is it?"

"Wolves, I 'spect. Storm's got 'em running in circles.
Better give 'em a shot to skedaddle." He went to the
fireplace and took down a high-powered rifle from
the rack. "I'll get Jude in. She'll bark herself hoarse
with a hunting pack in the vicinity." He took a frayed
parka from the peg beside the door, zipped it up

and chambered a round in the rifle. "Be back in a jif."

The Pathfinder leader fired at nearly point-blank range as the man came out of the cabin. He'd been flattened against the side of the cabin beside the door, four or five feet out of range of the dog's reach on its chain. The Husky was in a rage, up on its hind legs, straining against the tether, jumping, barking, its teeth flashing. The animal wasn't so excited that he was there, the Pathfinder guessed, as that he was there with a weapon. When the door opened, the Russian darted to one side, leveling the submachine gun about waist-high and fired half a clip into the stranger, which nearly cut him in half. He never saw the man's face. Another Pathfinder killed the dog as the leader and three others rushed inside. An old woman in a green robe turned toward him as he crashed in. Her expression was sudden surprise, not fright, and she began to raise a hand to her head when one of the others shot her. It was a quick burst. She was dead before she hit the floor.

In less than ten minutes the bodies were buried in a large drift behind the cabin and the bloodied snow shoveled away.

"Pathfinder patrol," the leader said in terse Russian into his hand radio. He sat in the same seat Arnold Jones had occupied fifteen minutes earlier. "Objective secure."

"Casualties?" It was the voice of Colonel Vorashin.

"Two noncombatants. Instructions?"

There was a pause, then: "Hold until contact."

## THE WHITE HOUSE 0859 HRS

The view from the Truman Balcony of the Rose Garden was one of crystalline bleakness; a glaze of frozen sleet encrusted all the trees, and they reflected the morning's gray, overcast light dully. President Thomas McKenna sat alone in his favorite easy chair with a cup of coffee balanced on one of its arms. Sections of the day's *New York Times* and *Washington Post* were strewn over a small side table from a stack of unread newspapers. McKenna chuckled at the political cartoon in the *Post*—a masked caricature of him wearing a battered white hat and empty six-gun holsters, sitting on a crate marked WHEAT and facing an angry Russian bear. The caption read: "No, no. I'm Kemosabe, *you're* the Indian."

Thomas Kyle McKenna was a forty-seven-year-old man who found humor where he could these days. As the forty-first president, he was neither generally beloved nor universally despised, depending upon whom you asked. Unlike his immediate predecessor he was exceptionally healthy, which was probably his single attribute that friend and foe could agree on without a congressional committee to verify. Not that it wasn't discussed. But Thomas McKenna's state of health wasn't so much an issue, he thought glibly, as was his state of mind. As vice-president for twenty-one months, he'd dropped out of sight, politically, as if he'd fallen down a very deep well. When President Daniel Churchill Thorpe died suddenly of a heart attack (Thorpe had been a vigorous sixty-six. While his death was certainly sudden, it was a monumental shock to the nation when it was eventually disclosed that this was his third attack in seventeen years), McKenna was hoisted out of the well and reexamined in the severe light of day. Nobody could prevent him from becoming president, though there were several party bosses who prayed that option was somehow available.

McKenna was most things Dan Thorpe had not been. He was young, a widower, not a war hero, liberal-minded and a former governor of a rural western state who had no congressional experience. He was sensitive and quietly intelligent where Thorpe had been simply smart and unbending the way a predatory animal is smart and lethal. But for precisely the reasons that he was unlike Thorpe, he was politically attractive for second slot on the presidential ticket. Thorpe had been "the Rock" and McKenna "the Face" ("the tits and ass element of Thorpe's traveling political show," one journalist had crudely dubbed McKenna during the campaign). After the election, Thorpe immediately began restructuring foreign policy with an eye to strengthening alliances, particularly NATO, in a move to check the Soviets. His reinstitution of the grain embargo had taken a heavy toll on the Russians in the wake of their worst grain harvest since the revolution. President Thorpe was born to face down the Russians, supporters had said. For the twenty-one months he lived in the White House, he was an ever-present challenge to their aggressions, and his announcement that he was seriously considering selling arms technology to the Chinese struck a raw Russian nerve. A test of wits and cunning was coming in this nuclear monopoly game, and Thorpe was the man to have on your side. Everybody knew that. Nobody dreamed he would die, of course. Now McKenna was president. It was a lousy trick, McKenna thought, him dying like that.

A short man hurried into the room. Wayne Kimball was always in a hurry. He had graduated first in his law class at Princeton in 1968, delivered the valedictory address and had been running ever since. He was an immaculate dresser with a decided preference for gray pin-striped suits which, he thought, befitted his station as White House chief of staff.

"Breakfast, Mr. President. Richard Hickman's already started in the study. If you want anything before he consumes it all, you'd better move your ass." Kimball took the coffee cup and saucer and set them on the stack of papers.

"That *was* my breakfast, Wayne."

"Up, please. Where's your jacket?"

McKenna pointed it out on the back of a chair. Kimball retrieved it and helped the president into the sleeves. "You're the chief of staff, Wayne, not a valet."

"I get no respect. C'mon. It's nine o'clock and—" Kimball stopped as McKenna turned toward him, staring at the president's tie. "Jesus Christ! Where did you shoot that thing?"

McKenna laughed. "Like it? Judge Stevenson picked it out."

"Out of what?" Kimball shook his head. "That lady may be a brilliant jurist and"—he shrugged—"and whatever else, but she hasn't got the slightest appreciation of what a presidential image should be."

"I guess that comes under the heading of separation of powers."

"Jokes? Jokes I get the first thing in the morning?"

McKenna buttoned his jacket. "So, what's on today? Soft, I hope."

"Nope." Kimball checked through a small leather-bound appointment book. "Briefing in twenty minutes, the regulars."

"Who's priority?"

"Farber, National Security."

"Jules Farber," McKenna said wearily. "I seem to spend my life with Jules Farber."

"Dick Hickman for breakfast," Kimball read from the notebook.

"And?"

"I suspect he wants you to announce."

"Too soon."

"Dick doesn't think so."

"Dick Hickman is a born campaign manager. That's the way he has to think. Luckily, he doesn't make the decisions. He'd have had me announcing the day Thorpe died, preferably the moment after I was sworn in."

"He thinks the great man is still president, you know. You're just sort of renting space until he returns."

"A lot of people have the same idea. When a president dies in office, especially someone like Dan Thorpe, people feel a terrifying loss, and they resent the poor schmuck who happens to be vice-president."

"You're not resented."

McKenna smiled. "I'd rather you'd said I wasn't a schmuck." He nodded at the notebook. "What else?"

"The devil's bitch at nine fifteen."

"Translate that, please."

"Dorothy Longworth. You promised her an interview and now it's time to pay up."

"It won't be that bad. She may be a vitriolic bitch, but she's a polite vitriolic bitch. Dick doesn't know she's here, I hope. He'd have a go at her skinny neck if he did."

"No, she's having coffee in the library. Stealing us blind, probably."

"Fine. Next?"

"Ad hoc committees on inflation."

"What do you bet they come in smiling to cover their long faces. 'The consumer price index,' Secretary

Bridges will say. 'Though it went up only two and a half percent last month, we have every reason to hope . . .' etcetera ad infinitum."

"You inherited inflation. You didn't invent it."

"The poor bastard who ten years ago thought he had a piece of the action has only got a bigger piece of the promise today. Inflation is running twenty percent. Remedy—a meeting. Alternative energy legislation is choking to death in . . . how many committees?"

"Eight in the Senate, twelve in the House."

"So what do I do? I meet with the Speaker and majority leader. What does it accomplish, Wayne? What?"

"What's the matter, reading editorials again?"

McKenna stared at the pile of newspapers. "They are the voices of the people, and the people aren't very happy."

"Sounds like *you've* been reading the vitriolic bitch's column."

"And others."

"Well, you know what I think—"

"Yes, I do." The president nodded impatiently at the appointment book. "Let's get on with it."

"Today is Gorny's birthday. You said you wanted to be reminded."

"Gorny?"

"Dimitri Gorny. Chairman Gorny. USSR Gorny. Horny-Gorny. The red-headed Ruskie with the eight-year-old kid."

"His son is ten, by the way. Let's send him a birthday greeting. I'll write out something after breakfast."

"I know what I'd like to send him."

"So do I."

"A twenty-five-megaton candle right up his—"

"Thank you, Wayne, but I have enough washroom warriors as it is." McKenna moved toward the door. "I may get slaughtered next November, but I do not intend to leave the next president of the United States a pile of hot ashes in lieu of a country." He stopped at the door. "Rescue me in about ten minutes. I don't think I can take too much of Dick Hickman this morning. Right?"

"You got it, boss." He glanced at his watch. "Go."

Richard Hickman was sixty, bald as an eagle, with the complexion of a boozer though he seldom drank. He was a huge man; he took up every inch of space in the delicate Queen Anne chair in the study. The sight of him sitting at the small breakfast table reminded McKenna of a character he'd seen in a children's storybook—Mr. Hippopotamus caught in the jaws of a whale, his big round eyes wide with terror.

McKenna walked briskly to the table. "Morning, Dick. Don't get up."

Hickman stuffed a slice of toast past his lips, nodding. "Morning, Mr. President," he managed to mumble.

McKenna sat down. He surveyed the damage his campaign manager had wrought on the breakfast meal. "You ate all the toast, you gluttonous bastard. You owe me two pieces of toast." He smiled in response to Hickman's startled look. Hickman never knew when he was being kidded. "Sorry I'm late, Dick. I keep letting Kimball schedule me to death. And before breakfast. Still, he does his job, which is why I keep him in gray suits. Everyone screaming crisis. So. I assume you're here to tell me to announce."

"I am." Hickman helped himself to more coffee.

"Why?"

"For the good of the country . . . the world."

"The universe," McKenna added with a warm smile. "C'mon, Dick."

"You have to declare now, Mr. President. People think you're losing your nerve. Some think you never stopped being vice-president. We need to make it emphatically clear that you intend to stay right here . . . right here in this historic house. Announce, Mr. President. Let me get to it."

"Ah, now the real reason is out. You're just looking for work."

"I *have* had other offers."

"Maybe you should take them up. The polls haven't been kind around here lately."

Now Hickman smiled. "I like a challenge."

"Acceptance polls bottom out at twenty-six percent? Anybody who enjoys odds like that *is* a masochist."

"I—*we* can turn that around. Just don't play an elusive game with the folks out there. Kennedy did that and you remember what happened to him. You've got to get out there and say—"

"I'm the best."

"You are."

McKenna leaned forward slightly. "You know, Dick, I might not even win the *party's* nomination."

"Pardon me, Mr. President, but that's horseshit. An incumbent president of the United States does not *lose* the bid for renomination."

"Ever heard of Chester Alan Arthur?"

"The twenty-first president? Are you quoting history now? That's my territory."

"I'm facing facts."

"Big deal. So it happened once. So what? You're not Chester Arthur and you're not being challenged by James Blaine. This isn't 1884, you know. *1*984 has enough stigma attached to it already. Don't look for more trouble."

McKenna shrugged. "You think Milt Weston has your appreciation of history?"

"If you'll excuse my saying so, Mr. President, but Senator Milton F. Weston hasn't got the brains God gave spiders. He's not going to run against *you*. He's not that stupid. It'd wreck the party, a fight like that. Oh, he'll make noises, he's good at that. But he'll stay in the Senate where he belongs. The ungrateful bastard. *You're* the one who put him there. You treated him like a kid brother."

"Well, now he's acting like one."

"What he needs is a swift kick in the ass."

"I can't really blame him, Dick," McKenna said,

glancing at his watch. "I believe *he* believes that I'm wrong for the country."

"I suppose you read what he said in the papers this morning? He's all hot air, but unless you begin some rebutting, people are going to start believing this drivel." Kimball read from a clipping. "'In Senator Weston's scathing denunciations of the president's newest tightening of the grain embargo of the Soviet Union, the erstwhile political ally and protégé of the president succeeded in demolishing the Administration's entire apologia for this self-defeating policy.'" He glanced up at the president. "Crap like this is what hurts."

"Our beloved Miss Longworth is using Milt to mangle me."

"She's an ass, Mr. President. But people *read* her tripe. She's a strong columnist, lots of papers pick her up. She wants you and Weston to destroy each other so her own candidate can pick up the jellybeans and move in here. Can you believe she's seriously backing Wes Nichols for president? Wes Nichols, for chrissake!"

"They call it freedom of choice, Dick. Nobody said you have to be smart to exercise it." McKenna watched him a moment. He'd been waiting for the right time. Now was perfect. "She's here, you know."

"Who is?"

"Dorothy. I'm seeing her right after I leave you."

Kimball nearly choked on his coffee. "Longworth!"

McKenna smiled broadly. "Right the first time."

"Oh, my." The campaign manager set his coffee down and closed his eyes. "Oh, my!"

"My loyal friends of the Fourth Estate depress me; they're so upset with everything. Mind you, they're correct in their depression. But our Miss Longworth feasts on despair and she tells me a lot. She doesn't know it, but her questions are their own answers."

Kimball exhaled a defeated breath. "You're the president, Mr. President."

"I'll get my resident economic genius started on a

rebuttal speech—that should please you. But that's it for now, Dick. I won't attack Senator Weston directly and I'm not ready to announce. Okay?"

"Well . . ."—Kimball let out a long sigh—". . . shit! All right. I guess you know what you're doing."

"If I don't Stu Fielding can make it sound as though I do. Isn't that what speechwriters and campaign managers are for?"

"I don't trust Stuart Fielding," Hickman said seriously. "He's ugly and horny. That's a bad combination." Then he smiled. "It's much better to be fat and bald."

The door to the study opened and Kimball looked in. "Mr. President, it's time for your nine-fifteen."

"Be right there. And, Wayne, put me down to see Stu Fielding sometime today. Short. I want a paper that shows positive results of our Soviet grain embargo. I want *our* farmers to understand . . . you know what I want."

Kimball was writing furiously. "Right. Brilliant speech. Embargo. Farm vote. I got it."

McKenna turned to Hickman. "Happy?"

"I'll be happy when you get me tickets to your next inaugural ball, Mr. President."

The president raised an eyebrow. He glanced at Kimball. "Won't we all."

Dorothy Longworth was perusing one of the volumes of Churchill's memoirs on World War II when the president joined her in the library. She was a small woman, oddly, McKenna thought, considering the clout she held in the press. He'd never actually noticed her height during press conferences as she was usually sitting down; she was not one of those jack-in-the-box correspondents of the White House Press Corps who competed for questions from the floor. She was thirty-five with a Dresden doll's face, and she dressed simply. She wore a dark, high-necked dress with her hair done up in a bun, an attempt, McKenna guessed, to make her appear older or more mature, perhaps both.

"Good morning, Miss Longworth," he said graciously. "I hope I haven't kept you waiting." He gestured for her to have a seat.

"Not at all, Mr. President." She set the book on a side table rather than putting it back in its place on the shelf. "I was just reading Mr. Churchill's reminiscences of the Potsdam meeting." She sat down in a flowered-print chair. "Did you ever meet him?"

"Churchill?" McKenna smiled. "I was eleven years old when they divided up Europe, Miss Longworth. I never even met Eisenhower." He took a seat opposite her on a matching love seat. "Do you know Walter Cronkite?"

Dorothy Longworth's mouth turned up slightly, her eyes half closed. "Touché." She took out a reporter's pad and pencil. "You know, Mr. President, I was a little surprised to get this interview."

"I figured it was about time we met face to face. As long as you're writing so much about my Administration, I thought you ought to meet the source of the country's problems."

Her eyes narrowed: "That isn't quite fair, Mr. President. It's not personal at all. My job is to write what I see. And I see an Administration in turmoil."

"Do you?"

"You're not getting much support from the Hill these days."

"What president *ever* got much support from Congress, Miss Longworth?"

She nodded and jotted quickly on her pad.

"One direct quote, sweetheart," McKenna said, pointing to her notebook, "and I'll paddle your ass right in the middle of my next press conference."

She glanced up sweetly. "I know the rules, Mr. President. I'm just generally noting the rich flavor of your thoughts."

"You couldn't *print* the rich flavor of my thoughts." He studied her severely. "No notes."

Dorothy Longworth sighed. She put her pencil down. "As you wish, then."

"Let's get down to it, shall we? What do you want?"

"That's direct."

"I don't know any other way. You came here for something exclusive, I assume."

"As a matter of fact—" She stopped and unfolded her hands. "Do you mind if I smoke, Mr. President?"

He shook his head. "Not at all. Are you nervous?"

"It's a journalist's bad habit. I have to have something to do with my hands. And if I can't take notes . . ."

"Light up."

She took a package of slim cigarettes from her purse and offered one to McKenna, who declined with a shake of his head.

"There *is* something on my mind," she said through a pale cloud of smoke as she extinguished the match.

"Shoot."

"Are you going to make a deal with Weston?" She leaned forward slightly.

"I have nothing to offer the senator," McKenna said casually. "Next question."

"The rumor is that if you step aside, hand him the nomination, you could return to Washington in any job you asked for."

"That *sounds* like a rumor."

"Is it true?"

"Aren't you counting your chickens a little early, Miss Longworth? Neither the senator nor I have made a commitment even to run for the nomination."

"Not publicly, no."

"I can't speak for the senator, and I wouldn't try to, but I haven't decided yet. You'll hear it when everyone else does."

"Weston is coming on strong. Any unquotable mellifluous comments?"

The president glanced at his watch. "Come on, Dorothy. Give me some tough questions. I have a

Security Council briefing in ten minutes. You make a fortune in syndication. Let me see you earn it."

"You *are* going to run again, aren't you?"

"I haven't run *yet*, if you'll recall."

"You're avoiding the question."

"Who wants to know, you or Wes Nichols?"

Her face turned angry. "I resent that! You have no right to ask—"

"As much right as you to print half-truths and rumors, my dear. Besides, this interview is off the record. You can tell me, Dorothy."

She composed herself quickly. "If you don't mind, Mr. President, I'll be the interviewer."

"What else do you want to know?"

"Oil," she said. "The *people* want to know about oil. Our supply is oozing to a halt from the Persian Gulf. What's really new on the Alaskan slopes?"

"New finds."

"Enough?"

"Hopefully."

"Gas rationing?"

"I'm still trying."

"It's *your* Congress, Mr. President."

"It's *our* Congress, ma'am. I don't appoint them, unfortunately. The people elect them. I just try to work with them. You ought to remember that."

"I do." She gave him a wicked smile. "I expect that's a thought heavy on your mind, too—the people voting, I mean."

McKenna grinned. "They told me you were a tiger."

"I expect they didn't say 'tiger,' either."

"No, tenacious bitch, actually. Yes, Miss Longworth, I'm aware that I wasn't elected to this job. *Everybody's* aware of it. It's not something I need reminding of. It doesn't bother me. If I run, I'll take my chances. If I don't—" He shrugged. "Like I said, you'll find out when I decide, just like everyone else."

"The polls don't look good for you. That doesn't bother you?"

"Polls?"

"C'mon, Mr. President."

"Lyndon Johnson's polls didn't look good either, in 1963. But he won by the biggest margin in history the next year."

"You're not running against Barry Goldwater."

McKenna chuckled to himself. "Some people think I *am* Barry Goldwater."

"What about the Russians?"

"What about them?"

"SALT. I'm talking about SALT . . . the talks, the embargo. When are you going to sit down with them again?"

"I'm ready. They're not."

"What does that mean?"

"Just what it's always meant, Miss Longworth," McKenna said wearily. "When they pull their troops out of Afghanistan, when they drive their tanks out of Poland, when they stop trying to slice up Yugoslavia, when they quit their aggressions in countries that don't want them . . . then we can talk."

"And the embargo?"

"Continues."

"Russians are starving."

"Would you like to know how many Poles or Afghans were shot last week?"

"Now you sound like President Thorpe."

"I inherited a foreign policy that the people wanted. They still want it."

"The farmers aren't crazy about it."

"Did you ever hear Lincoln's epigram about pleasing the people?"

"Now you sound callous."

The president got up slowly from his seat. "I guess there isn't any pleasing you, is there, Miss Longworth?"

"I didn't come to be pleased, just to get some straight answers."

"Are you satisfied?"

"Are you?"

"I'm never satisfied, Miss Longworth. Never. I just get older." He checked his watch once more. "I'm afraid I'm out of time. I hope this meeting was of some use to you. I certainly enjoyed it."

"You're a gracious liar, Mr. President."

"You weren't a disappointment, either, ma'am. Tenacity fits you rather well, I think."

"Bitch, too, probably."

McKenna smiled. "Probably."

He walked quickly to his desk in the Oval Office. Kimball was at his heels.

"Well, was she everything I said she was?" he asked anxiously.

"I don't think she got quite what she was after," McKenna said. He took off his jacket and stretched his back. He went to the window and stared out at the gloom of day.

"What did she want?"

"Same thing they all want, Wayne." He spoke slowly, tiredly. "I wish I could go fishing," he said after a long pause. "I'd really like that. A week with a fly rod and hip boots and no Air Force colonel following me around with launch codes in his little black case."

"You're the president of the United States. You don't get vacations."

"Lucky me."

"They're waiting," Kimball said. "In the conference room."

"Yes, my little shadow Jules Farber and the rest of the wise men."

"C'mon, you're already behind schedule today. You can feel sorry for yourself tonight, cry in your pillow. This morning you have to be commander in chief."

McKenna turned to face his chief of staff. "Sometimes you can be a real prick, Wayne. I guess that's why I like you so much."

"I love it when you talk dirty, Mr. President." Kimball held the president's coat. "C'mon."

McKenna bent his knees as Kimball helped him on

with his coat. "You know, sometimes I think that somewhere out there in space, on some distant planet, creatures are studying our world with a kind of terrible sadness."

"Well, if they are so smart, why don't they send us something we can use—like an instant IQ analyzer gun. Something we can use to expose all the fools on this place."

The president laughed. "What, and put me out of a job?" He shook his head and was suddenly serious. "No, we don't need more idiots, Wayne. We need something more useful than another gun. Something more important."

"Yeah." Kimball walked him to the door. "Like what, for instance?"

"Like missionaries," McKenna replied. "What we need are missionaries."

The Eskimo squad reached the runway ahead of schedule by twenty-two minutes. Ten US Army Scouts of the Alaskan National Guard 11th Regiment. They had been out now twelve hours on a competitive training maneuver with three other squads who'd taken different routes on a timed exercise of map reading and arctic survival. They were on snowshoes with packs and skis on their backs and they carried M-16s. Unloaded.

Corporal Paul Avalik, the radioman, stopped when the squad leader held up his hand. He noticed the wind sock standing stiff in a hard wind. They'd been walking ninety minutes since their last break and Avalik was dying for a cigarette.

The squad leader shuffled awkwardly to Avalik. "We're early," he yelled against the wind in his face. Avalik could see the outline of a smile beneath the face protector and goggles of his squad leader. Winning the training maneuver—that is, returning to the company before the other squads—was all his sergeant cared about, Avalik thought. What he cared about was getting home and taking a nice warm pee.

"Right," the corporal said.

"We'll get time confirmation from Jones, then head back to base." The sergeant ducked his head against the wind a moment, then added, "We'll beat Parsons and his bunch by a good half hour."

It was too cold to answer. Avalik nodded. Who gives a shit anyway, he thought. The squad leader made another gesture, swinging his arm forward. "Move out." He was a regular John Wayne freak, his sergeant was.

They moved down the center of the runway toward the cabin. Avalik could hear the wind whistling past the Quonset hut ahead. He hoped Mrs. Jones had coffee made. He knew his sergeant wouldn't wait if it wasn't already made. He pictured the Joneses' cabin in his mind: the kitchen, the pot-bellied stove, the mass of radio gear next to the fireplace. A warm, cozy little place. Yeah, she'd have coffee brewing, he was certain. What else was there to do up here on a day like this?

Avalik saw the shape outside the cabin. He didn't know if he was the first to see it because nobody else seemed to notice. The corporal had been looking for Jones's dog, and he saw the shape of a man standing in the small indention where the cabin and Quonset hut came together. There wasn't anything surprising about it, Jones was probably outside, but they were very near the cabin now and the dog should have been barking his head off. Still, they were walking with their backs to the wind and the snow was blowing . . .

He was wearing white arctic gear, and Avalik heard his sergeant mutter some curse. It was some jerk from one of the other squads, Avalik thought. They'd got lost and gone to Jones's place to find their bearings. He saw another figure. Then another. They were all around the cabin holding their weapons in front of them. Stupid nitwits. Why weren't they inside where it was warm. Why hadn't they . . .

They started shooting all at once. The squad leader

went down first as he was at the point, the back of his white parka suddenly red with blood from three gaping exit wounds. The soldier directly in front of Avalik windmilled backward, his M-16 falling away from him. And then everyone was falling. The stiff arctic wind was loud with men screaming, whirling awkwardly in their snowshoes as they died stumbling into one another. Avalik was hit on the right hand; the slug ripped off his canvas mitten and twirled him around so that he suddenly faced into the wind, gasping for breath. The second bullet pierced his left leg above the knee. He fell face down in the snow. He'd kicked off both snowshoes and started rolling when the real massacre began. The sound of automatic weapons thundered all around him. The bullets made the snow dance, white sprays which were consumed by the swirling wind and transformed the patch of runway into a white nightmare of death. Avalik tried rolling again and was hit in the side by a ricochet. Another slug destroyed the radio on his back and shattered one of his skis. He scrambled on all fours, mindless of the pain of his wounds, desperate only to get out of the lines of fire.

Unable to see and afraid to stop, Avalik ran like a crippled spider until he dropped headfirst off the edge of the runway. He rolled behind a mogul and stopped. The shooting continued for another thirty seconds though the screams had already ceased. He waited, his mouth clamped shut against the burning pain in his leg and side. He waited, afraid to look back toward the runway to see one of the figures in white coming for him. He waited, but nothing happened. When the shooting ended, there was nothing. Only the wind.

*"Podshchitai i zakapai."*

The disembodied voice came from out of the whiteness. Avalik didn't move. He held his breath, expecting to be kicked or to hear the short static cough from an automatic weapon that would end his misery permanently. But he wasn't kicked or shot and he didn't hear the voice again. For half an hour he just lay there. His white parka would serve as some camouflage, and if the blowing snow covered the blood that was surely splattered over his legs, they might not find him. He fought against the urge to cry out for help. He tried to orient himself. He prayed.

When he'd gotten enough nerve to raise his head, he saw nothing but swirling snow. He rolled onto his back and nearly blacked out from the pain. It took nearly another half hour to apply a compress from his first-aid kit on his leg and untangle himself from the straps and buckles of his radio and cartridge belt. He didn't know where his rifle was—he didn't even remember dropping it—but he wasn't going to need it anyway. Not against those guys.

Corporal Avalik started crawling. He knew approximately where he was and approximately where he had to go. The main thing was to get away. That was the first thing. *Stay alive* and pray he could make his way back to the company. They'd send a squad looking, sooner or later. Maybe . . . maybe he could walk, at least hobble along, once he was safely away from here. But that was something to think about later.

He didn't think about the Russians. He didn't think about them, but he knew that's what they were from the moment he heard the voice. It didn't matter to him and he didn't care *why* they were there, though it was pretty obvious. All he had to worry about now was not freezing to death and staying alive until someone else found him. *Then* he could worry about the Russians.

Avalik reached out with both hands and pulled himself forward. Snow whipped at his face. Just one foot at a time, he thought. Just one foot at a time.

# MOSCOW 0900 HRS

The short procession of cars, a black limousine sand-wiched between a pair of unmarked sedans, moved cautiously through the falling snow like three near-sighted beetles. It was Party Chairman Dimitri Gorny's daily routine. He drove his son to school every morning and the security cars led-followed him everywhere he went like worker ants protecting their queen.

Gorny was in the rear seat of the limousine with his son Aram, a slight, gentle boy dressed in a school uniform and wearing a heavy coat. The physical differences between father and son were striking. Gorny was powerfully built; his thick neck was merely an extension of his shoulders and his strong, disciplined face seldom gave away the workings of his mind. They were logical characteristics for a man party members had nicknamed The Bull. It was a name Gorny himself found amusing. He considered himself more thoughtful than bullish, more patient than headstrong, though there were times when it was expedient to let the party members believe what they wished.

Aram sat up in the seat, craning for a glimpse of the car that followed them. He'd been quieter than usual this morning, Gorny thought. In the last weeks his lessons had taken on the mysteries of planetary space and these morning rides were full of questions. The boy had decided to become a cosmonaut, and his energy on the subject was boundless. Except today.

"Those cars, Papa," Aram said, pointing to one out the rear window. "Could they really help us if anything happened?"

Gorny frowned. He'd long ago given up trying to understand the motivation behind his son's inquisitiveness. The chairman nodded. "Of course."

Aram gave him that how-do-you-know look.

Gorny tapped the window separating the front compartment from the rear. Major Veich, his personal bodyguard, turned quickly in the passenger seat and slid the glass back. "Yes, comrade Chairman?"

"Our friends, front and rear"—Gorny indicated with his head—"could they really help us if anything happened? Aram is interested."

The major looked at the boy with a smile. "Of course."

"How?" Aram asked innocently.

"Well . . ." Veich let his glance touch the most powerful man in the Soviet Union. Gorny knew that look. It said why do you do this to me. "Well, they'd stop immediately, of course."

"And?" Gorny tried not to smile.

"I mean, those men would be all over us before anything *could* happen," Veich explained. "They are trained especially for this work, little one."

The chairman turned to his son. "I think they could not do much, either."

"I'd protect you, Papa."

Gorny nodded proudly. "Yes, but you have more serious thoughts to consider in school than heroic fantasies."

"They'd have to kill me first," the boy said.

"Please stop having us all killed," Gorny said. When

he glanced at the major, Veich was smiling. "The boy dreams of such terrors."

*"You* speak of terror, Papa."

Not only inquisitive but a parrot, Gorny thought. "In another context, Aram," he said, slightly annoyed. To Veich he said, "His mother allows him too many films."

"Yes," the major said, amused, "mine also."

The procession slowed for a bus that had been stopped by something up ahead. Veich spoke quickly into a hand microphone, instructing the driver of the lead car not to stop. "Move around it, then," he said in response to an apparently lame explanation. He turned back to Gorny. "A commotion ahead, comrade Chairman. We will be past it in a moment."

The commotion was a swarm of police with dogs and truncheons chasing a crowd of students. The limousine sped up in pace with the lead sedan but not before Gorny saw a woman lying on the sidewalk bleeding heavily from an open gash across her forehead. Several of the students were throwing rocks and the police waded into them, clubs swinging. Aram saw it, too.

"Papa, what are they doing?" He jumped up on the seat, following the action through the rear window as the car sped off. "What were they doing?"

"Hooligans," Veich said quickly, ". . . loafers. They disgrace their country."

Gorny glanced wearily at his bodyguard. "Please, Major, no clichés in front of my son." He pulled Aram back into the seat by the hem of his coat. "Sit down, please. It is not a matter that demands your concern."

"But, Papa? The police, they were—"

"It is a difficult time, Aram. People behave badly sometimes. Even good people. Sometimes."

The boy nodded as if he understood. "But you are correcting things, aren't you, Papa? *You* are." He beamed a smile and quoted a line he'd been taught was truth. "'All things are correctable.'"

Gorny looked away. He studied the gray street. "All things are correctable," he said quietly. "Of course." He leaned closer to Major Veich and spoke in a low voice so his son could not hear. "I would like some people added to the school detail, Major." He was wearing his bull face.

"I have already done so, comrade Chairman," Veich replied with matching grimness. "Today."

The chairman's official Kremlin office was so large no amount of furniture could make it appear less than grand. It was the ceilings, Gorny had commented the first time he'd seen it; they were too high and the windows were too large. It made the place too hot in summer and too cold in winter, but it was the party chairman's traditional office and he used it only on official occasions or when he met with party members who expected no less than grand surroundings in which to conduct party business. The office he preferred was a smaller adjoining room which had been renovated and modernized (including a lower ceiling) and was more comfortable for the day-to-day affairs of state. This morning's briefing, unfortunately, brought him to the official office, where he sat at the head of a ridiculously large conference table. Around it were seated Premier Sergei Temienko, age seventy, whose halting habits of speech were incessantly irritating (he paused between words as if out of courtesy for someone to write them down—assuming anyone wanted to); Foreign Minister Anatol Venchikof, age sixty; Minister of Agriculture Nadia Kortner, age forty-eight, though there was some doubt; Marshal of the Army Viktor Budner—in uniform, of course—age seventy-five, who invariably had difficulty seeing across such a wide expanse of table to follow whoever happened to be speaking; and Colonel General Aleksey Rudenski, age fifty, head of the KGB and the most dangerous man present. Of all of them, Gorny distrusted Rudenski most.

For the moment, Gorny wasn't troubled by the collected powers around the table before him. He was laughing. He was laughing so hard that tears streamed down his face while the others only stared solemnly in his direction, looking at the cable he held between his hands. The sound of his laughter echoed in the large, chilly room.

"Comrade Chairman," Venchikof said from his place several seats away, "what has the fascist American president said that so amuses you?"

Gorny wiped his eyes. "Granted, McKenna is a fascist and an imperialistic sonofabitch, but the man does have humor." He held up the cable to read. "'On behalf of the people of the United States, I would like to extend my heartiest congratulations on the occasion of the anniversary of your birth. . . .'" He looked around the table. "Not my birthday, comrades, 'the *anniversary* of my birth.' He speaks as if I were a war memorial." He continued reading. "'Even with the unfortunate difficulties that face our two countries today, one has to respect anyone who can survive another year in high office without abandoning dedication to freedom, justice, prosperity and, most of all, a never-ending search for a permanent and lasting peace.'" Gorny set the cable down, smiling and shaking his head.

"Very amusing," Nadia Kortner said. She didn't smile.

Gorny sat down. "I know McKenna. He wrote that cable himself. Shall I translate it for you, comrades?"

Marshal Budner squinted down the table. He was even farther away than Venchikof. "It *has* been translated," he said.

"Not really, my dear Marshal. What the president has said to me—to all of us—is that it's a miracle we've all lasted here . . . from one birthday to another. He is also reminding us that *we* are in as much trouble as *he* is."

*"We,"* Rudenski said quietly, "are not *in* any trouble."

Marshal Budner sat up. "What?" He glanced at the foreign minister. "What was that?"

Venchikof ignored the marshal. "Let him have his

joke. I promise you that he will not be laughing next year. He will no longer be president next year."

Gorny considered it. "Perhaps. But then, perhaps, better a devil we know than one we don't."

"If we *might* bring this discussion back to current events," Nadia Kortner said. She opened the large red folder in front of her and continued. "I have received the latest report on American farming. The number of bankruptcies of farmers holding a hundred acres or less has risen thirty-eight percent in one year—their grain embargo is a catastrophe."

"You are very good at numbers, Madame Kortner," Gorny said lazily, "but I wonder if you realize who is suffering most." To all of them he said, "The Central Committee meets in a week's time. We are only three months away from the Thirty-Eighth Congress and, in my opinion, we are never farther away from disaster than yesterday."

Prime Minister Temienko nodded. "Granted, there are some stresses, but—"

"You call our problems *stresses?*" Gorny put on his bull face. "I saw something this morning in the streets of Moscow—police beating students. In Moscow! We are facing more than stresses, I think."

"I'm sorry about that, comrade Chairman," Rudenski said in a tone that was not apologetic. "Those revanchist hooligans will not be seen on the streets of Moscow ever again."

"Can your KGB guarantee it, Rudenski?" Gorny turned to him angrily. "Can the KGB guarantee no more food riots in the Ukraine? No more outbreaks in Bessarabia? No danger of the further disintegration of the Warsaw Pact? No problems with our armies in—"

"Please, comrade Chairman!" Marshal Budner rose from his chair. "The loyalty of every unit of the Soviet Armed Forces is not even open to question."

"*I* question it," Gorny shot back. "Don't be naive, my dear Marshal. You know we have been beseiged by reports of desertions."

"Every army has them," Budner replied. "They are

the criminals, the drunkards, the antiparty opportunists in certain units. It is nothing of great—"

"Please spare me," Gorny said. "Sit down, Marshal."

Budner began to object. "But—"

*"Please,"* said The Bull.

Budner took his seat, scratching it across the floor in childish protest.

Gorny stood, then paced behind his chair. "Comrades, you are all intelligent people. When we meet privately you are honest, frank, blunt"—he glanced at Venchikof—"and caring. Why is it that whenever you are gathered together you are mindless of mistakes, of conceding errors, of acknowledging problems?" The large room was silent as he walked to a large window and stared into the cobblestone street. "There was a time, comrades, when that square was brimming with traffic. Even in the dead of winter. People, cars, buses—activity that reflected an energetic and vigorous city. Now . . ." He sighed. "Now, except for a few bundled passersby and the looming Byzantine spires of St. Basil's, the square exudes little more than pronounced desolation."

"Comrade Chairman." It was Venchikof's high-pitched voice. "When you present your redevelopment program to the Central Committee—"

Gorny swung back to face the table. "If the world perceives us as a stricken cartoon, announcements of dozens of five-year plans will not change our image."

"There is only one perception that matters these days," Rudenski said. He nodded down the table toward Marshall Budner. "The Soviet might. We are not simply sickle and hammer, comrade. Somehow that image is lost in your assessments. *No one* has any misconception of the potency of the Soviet military or its supremacy."

"Truly spoken," Gorny said. "But if we have to *prove* our military superiority, we have failed, comrade Rudenski."

The head of the KGB nodded politely. "A matter of

opinion, I think, comrade Chairman." He glanced at Gorny with a measured look.

"Have you a solution to our dilemma then?"

Rudenski half smiled. He pursed his lips. "I'm working on it, comrade Chairman," he said. "I'm working on it."

## FORT WAINWRIGHT
## FAIRBANKS, ALASKA 1530 HRS

Jake Caffey stepped off the transport plane into a coldness that singed his lungs with his first breath. Snow and wind whipped his face and caused his eyes to water as he fought his way towards the operations office. Outside the door was a sign for newcomers.

WELCOME TO FORT WAINWRIGHT
HOME OF THE YUKON COMMAND
171ST INFANTRY BRIGADE
GEN. G. F. ROBERTS, COMMANDING

Caffey caught his breath. When his eyes had cleared he stared through the frosted window at the desolate runway and the ominous gray clouds that seemed to hang low enough to touch. He blew on his hands. He knew it was cold in Alaska, but Jesus Christ . . .

"Colonel Caffey?"

Caffey turned around to find a large master sergeant standing before him.

"Welcome to Wainwright, Colonel," the sergeant said. He handed Caffey a new arctic parka. "You'll find you'll need this, sir. That overcoat might be good back home, but it ain't worth a damn up here, sir."

"Thank you. Sergeant . . . ?"

"Bufford, sir. Melvin Bufford. Brigade command NCOIC. I have a jeep to take you to your quarters, Colonel."

Caffey changed from his overcoat to the parka. "Jeeps run up here, do they?" He was only half joking.

"Only for very short runs." The sergeant smiled. "We use snowcats otherwise. It does get a little chilly in the winter hereabouts for normal vehicles."

Caffey zipped the parka closed. "And how chilly is it now?"

The sergeant shrugged. "Not too bad, sir. About twenty-five, thirty below."

M/Sgt. Bufford drove. The streets, Caffey noted with mild surprise, were paved and relatively clear of snow. Fort Wainwright was not a large post, and that fact was noticeable in the few buildings Caffey saw until Bufford explained that most of the operations offices and all of the personnel quarters were below ground. It wasn't for strategic reasons, the sergeant said, it was simply for logical cost-efficiency—underground buildings were a fraction of the cost to heat than aboveground buildings. It had only taken the army forty years to see that.

Caffey's quarters were in Sub Block B3, No. 16. It wasn't enormous, but it was meticulously clean. Bufford took him on a tour of the rooms—two bedrooms, a kitchen with all built-ins including a microwave oven, a living room and a small den. The beds were made, the bathroom was furnished with towels and complimentary medicine-cabinet items, the pantry shelves were lined with canned goods and the refrigerator was stocked with the usual things, including a six-pack of beer.

The sergeant's tour ended in what was meant to be

the master bedroom. It didn't have a separate bath-room, and without windows it seemed much smaller than it really was. Caffey sat on the edge of the bed. "Very nice, Sergeant Bufford."

"Well, it isn't North Carolina, Colonel, but I think you'll be comfortable."

"Where on earth did those come from?" Caffey pointed to a vase of fresh flowers on the dresser. "Flowers? Up here?"

"Oh, well, they're from Mrs. Roberts, sir. The general's fixed her up with a hothouse in their quarters . . . artificial lights, special soil . . ." He shrugged. "She sends them around to most of the offices here, sir." His mouth hinted at a smile. "Every day."

Caffey nodded. "I see."

"General Roberts is expecting you at 1800 hours, Colonel. In his quarters. He's having several of the officers over for an informal wel—"

"Yes, I know."

"Shall I have a driver standing by, sir?"

"Where are the general's quarters?"

"Sub Block A1."

"Which number?"

"There isn't any," Bufford said. "I mean, SB-A1 *is* his quarters."

"The whole block?"

"Yes, sir."

Caffey lay on the bed. He closed his eyes and put an arm over his forehead. "Yes, please have a driver, Sergeant. And a map of the post, if there is one. If not, draw one up. I want to know where everything is and how to get to it. After today I won't need a driver or a jeep."

"Yes, sir."

"Is my office in one of these caves?" He smiled, glancing up at the sergeant.

"Yes, sir."

Caffey nodded. "Fine."

"You'll get used to it, Colonel. Anyway, there isn't much to see even if you could look outside."

"I'll adjust."

Bufford pointed out the phone on the end table beside the bed. "My extension is three-nine-six, Colonel. If you need anything—"

"No, thanks. I'm going to take a nap, then have a hot shower."

"Yes, sir." The sergeant turned to leave, stopped and turned back. "Oh, I almost forgot, Colonel." He reached inside his parka. "This came for you about two hours ago." He handed Caffey a folded telegram envelope.

Caffey slit it open with his fingernail, read it, then nodded to himself.

"I hope it isn't bad news, sir," Bufford said. His face registered genuine concern. "You've had enough of a shock for one day."

"No," Caffey said. "Not *bad* news. Nothing unexpected, anyway."

Bufford nodded. "We *are* glad to have you with us, Colonel. When I saw the orders that *you* were coming, sir, well, I . . ." He ducked his head slightly, suddenly embarrassed. "It's good to have an officer of your experience and background. You'll find these are good men here at the one-seventy-first, Colonel Caffey. The best."

"I didn't expect otherwise, Sergeant," Caffey said with a smile. "Thanks for the moral support. I'll be fine once I'm settled in."

"Yes, sir."

Caffey waited to hear the door close before he read the telegram again.

> DIANE AND I NOT MOVING ALASKA. SURE
> YOU UNDERSTAND. CALL WHEN CAN.
> DON'T EXPECT TO CHANGE MIND. DIANE
> SENDS LOVE. (SIGNED) NANCY.

He wondered how long it had taken her to compose it. That she sent a telegram rather than tell him face-to-face didn't surprise him; Nancy never was good at confrontations. But she was thrift-minded; the telegram word count came in at under the maximum allowed before the rate changed. He looked at the message again. Those twenty-one words effectively characterized the state of his marriage.

Caffey put the telegram back in the envelope and set it on the table beside the telephone. He lay back on the pillow and stared at the ceiling. "Oh, shit," he said in a low voice.

Brigadier General Gard Fitzgerald Roberts was a man Nancy could identify with, Caffey thought, when he arrived at the general's quarters. Although restricted by the architectural limitations of underground living, it looked like a general's home. It still had that distinctive air of army issue about it—that Spartan look of assignment-living that you knew could all be packed up in half a day if necessary—but it had the *feel* of a general-grade officer's residence. There were lots of framed photographs of Roberts at different ranks with high-ranking officers and politicians; one was with the Army Chief of Staff taken obviously in a Pentagon office, and another, in a large brushed-metal frame, with a large group of officers posed around President Nixon—Roberts was fourth from the president, on the right.

There were too many Gard Robertses in the military, Caffey had long believed. It was just his misfortune to be assigned to serve under one. He knew the kind of commander Roberts was and, by his manner, Roberts knew he knew. That they understood each other made for an awkward reception. They were polite, but their courtesies veiled an underlying acrimony neither of them could deny.

"This was very kind of you, General," Caffey was saying. They were standing near Roberts's wet bar, each with a drink. The cocktail party had broken up into small groups. A private in cook's whites passed with a tray of hors d'oeuvres. Except for the uniform,

Caffey had done this less than twelve hours ago. He appreciated it even less.

"Delete the 'General' tonight, Caffey. You have the rest of your tour for that." Roberts was uncomfortable and slightly inebriated. He seemed unsure how he should handle his new deputy commander. "Enjoy yourself."

"I think I'd call you General if I ran into you in a Juneau whorehouse, General. It's a habit that's hard to break." Caffey tried to smile. He hated this ridiculous chitchat.

"Careful of your references, Caffey," Roberts said, half severely. "Don't want the ladies to get the wrong impression." He laughed too loudly.

Caffey nodded. Jesus Christ, he thought.

Mrs. Roberts introduced herself again and offered Caffey an appetizer. She was slightly taller than her husband with a more intelligent face. She'd also had a few more drinks.

"It's *so* nice to have you, Colonel Caffey. Is your wife coming soon?" She leaned against her husband slightly for support.

"Not right away, I'm afraid, Mrs. Roberts."

"Oh, call me Clare, Colonel."

Caffey imitated a smile. "Clare."

"Did you get the flowers?"

"Yes. They're beautiful."

"I grow them, you know. I have—"

"I don't think Caffey has a great abiding interest in flowers," Roberts said impatiently. "Anyway, I want some time with him."

Caffey saw the tiny flicker of hurt in her eyes, but it passed. She's used to it, he thought. He wondered what it was like to live with a man like that—the pompous sonofabitch. Then he thought it probably wasn't much different from what Nancy had to endure.

Clare moved off after gracefully detaching herself from them and Roberts motioned Caffey to a corner of the living room under a color photograph of himself in a dress uniform.

"Caffey, we have a very smooth operation here. That's how I want it to stay—smooth."

"I'm all for that, General."

"I want you to know that I didn't ask for you here."

Caffey nodded. "I appreciate your directness."

"This isn't the 81st Airborne. We do things differently up here. That means you do what *I* tell you to do *when* I tell you to do it. I don't like initiative, Caffey. Initiative is disruptive. You're deputy brigade commander, and I emphasize the deputy. Is that plain enough to you?"

"Loud and clear, General."

"Good." Roberts let out a sigh. He even smiled. "You can make full bird colonel with me, Caffey, if you don't rock the boat. It's not a flashy command, but it *is* visible to the Pentagon. If you're smart, that should be important to you."

"Doing my job is what's important to me, General."

"Just remember our little talk. I—" Something caught Roberts's eye. He looked up over Caffey's shoulder and smiled broadly, gesturing with his hand. "Now, there's an officer that stands out in this man's army."

She'd just entered and her cheeks were pink from the cold. Several officers greeted her. Mrs. Roberts took her coat and offered her an appetizer. She was in uniform. The rank was major now, up from second lieutenant six years ago.

"Katie," Caffey said softly, almost stunned.

"You know Major Breckenridge?" Roberts said.

"I knew her." He set his drink down. "Norfolk. She was the youngest instructor attached to the Code and Cipher School."

"She's *my* S-2 chief now," Roberts said proudly. "Best damned intelligence officer I've ever had. And ambitious. Wainwright is just a pit stop for her."

Caffey nodded. "So was Norfolk," he said under his breath.

She made her way through a tangle of officers to where Roberts and Caffey stood. Her eyes never left

Caffey. "Hello, Jake," she said when she was near enough to touch him. The general might as well have been invisible. "Long time."

Caffey nodded. "Long time."

For several seconds neither of them spoke. They just stared at each other. Finally, Roberts interrupted with a bright observation.

"So, you know each other, do you?"

Major Breckenridge broke away first. She gave the general a dazzling smile. "Yes, General. Maj—I mean, Colonel Caffey was one of my first students at Command and Staff. I was just out of the Point, and my first duty was teaching field-grade officers theory on the new PRC-82 intelligence coder." She shook her head and glanced at Caffey. "It was a little intimidating, a brand new second luey surrounded by all that brass."

"You got over it, I hope," Caffey said.

"More or less." She turned to Roberts. "I could use a drink, General. Where do I drop my quarter?"

Roberts gestured with his head. "That way."

"Mind if I buy one for our new recruit? I won't tell him any secrets."

"No, go ahead." To Caffey he said, "We've had our talk, haven't we, Colonel?"

"Yes, sir."

Kate slung an arm inside Caffey's and led him to the wet bar. She dropped ice into a pair of glasses. "Still bourbon straight up?"

"Yeah." He glanced around for eavesdroppers. "*I* didn't know you were here."

She continued making the drinks. "I've known for a week. I figured sooner or later we'd bump into each other again." She handed him his bourbon. "Drink to old times, Ma—God, I'll have to get that right— Colonel?"

He took a long sip. "You still make them too strong."

"You haven't changed, either. Still tough as nails and twice as mean."

"And older."

"Any wiser?" She took a long swallow of her drink. "How do I look? Tough, mean or old?"

"Taller," Caffey said. He smiled. "You look good, Katie. Very good."

"Where's Nancy?"

A captain moved in to pour two scotch and waters. He made some slurred comment about drinking while the moon was full and laughed to himself. When he was gone Kate's expression had not changed.

"Is it a sore subject?"

"What?" Caffey said. He tried not looking at her.

"Mrs. Caffey."

"She's not coming this trip," he said finally. "She doesn't have a sealskin coat." He glanced at her and tried to shrug it off but it didn't work.

"Trouble?"

Caffey sighed into his glass. "It isn't important. Okay?"

"Whatever you say, Colonel." She put her glass down and waved at someone across the room. "Listen, Jake, I'm going to be social for about"—she glanced at her watch—"ten minutes. Then I'm going to get a headache or something and leave this boring little shindig. I have a jeep upstairs. If you want to talk or just ride in measured silence, it's up to you."

"Look, you don't have—"

"Ten minutes." She got up to leave. "Unless you have a better offer."

Caffey shook his head. "Six years hasn't dampened your determination. Do you ever *not* get what you want?"

"Once every six years or so."

"Where're we going?"

She smiled. "Backward."

It was colder when he came out, even with some drinks in him, than when he went in, Caffey thought, as he trod out into the bitter night's stillness. He glanced around, keeping the parka hood drawn tight, and was momentarily blinded by the headlights of the jeep.

"C'mon, get in!" Kate yelled from inside the canvas cab as the four-wheeled vehicle pulled up beside him.

Caffey pulled back the door flap and hopped in. "Jesus! I never knew such cold!"

She shifted into gear and the jeep lurched forward. Over the roar of the engine, she said, "Patience, Colonel. I'll unfreeze you soon enough."

"Determined, promoted *and* randy. That's a dangerous combination, Major. Don't you have a stud up here?"

"Got shipped to Meteorological Research in Seattle last month," she said, keeping her eyes on the road. She nearly had to yell to be heard above the engine. "Just as well, though. He slept too much." She glanced over at him. "You still good in bed?"

The jeep hit a bump that jarred Caffey's teeth. His head bounced against the canvas top.

"I didn't hear you, Jake."

"I didn't say any—"

"What?"

"Yes," he yelled. "And better!"

She gave him a knowing look. "We'll see."

Her place was exactly the same as his only reversed. It wasn't particularly feminine, but nothing was in the army. They shed their parkas at the door and embraced in a long kiss in the center of the living room. For some inexplicable reason, Caffey felt enormously guilty. Just like the last time.

Kate slid away from him slowly. She rested her head against his chest. "Should we put a log in the fireplace and talk or go directly to bed and talk afterward?"

"You don't expect much, do you?"

"After six years?" She looked up at him. "You didn't even call."

"What, and tell you I was going home to Nancy? That would have made it easier for us, wouldn't it?"

"I loved you."

"And I had a seven-year-old daughter. Losing you

was the price for keeping her. The choice wasn't even close."

She pulled away from him and moved to the wood bin. "The log-in-the-fire option was my second preference, actually."

"Look, maybe I should just go. This isn't the best time for me to be digging up old memories."

"Digging up?" Kate's eyes flashed. "I didn't get a chance the *last* time! Nancy made all the decisions for us. Well, she isn't here, Colonel! We can play out this match head-to-head!"

"Goddamnit, Kate, I don't want to fight you!"

"Then we'd better settle things now! I'm willing to forget six years. That's one hell of a fucking commitment! What are you willing to do?"

For several moments he only stared at her. She was on the verge of tears, he knew her well enough to see that, but her pride wouldn't allow her to cry in front of him. Not now, not yet.

Of the thousand things he wanted to say to her, to share with her, to feel with her, it was ultimately what he *had* to do that made him move. It wasn't necessary that he say anything. All he had to do was leave.

Caffey found his parka beside the door. Wherever Sub Block B3 No. 16 was, it was going to be a long, cold walk.

# BROOKS MOUNTAIN RANGE 2345 HRS

He rested in a depression behind a mogul that shielded him from the violence of the blowing snow. In the last couple of hours the weather had changed, and not for the better. He didn't mind the wind so much or the darkness, he'd done this kind of dead reckoning before in worse storms. He wasn't lost, exactly. He knew which direction this sort of storm was coming from and therefore he had some idea which direction to head. After all, he was an Eskimo, and Eskimos don't get lost up here. At least, that was the accepted notion.

Corporal Avalik tied another compress around his leg wound. That was the problem—in all the snow and wind and darkness he couldn't see how badly it was bleeding, or *if* it was still bleeding, beneath the arctic trousers leg. He couldn't do anything about the bullet hole in his side. He figured it wasn't bleeding, at least it wasn't bleeding much, because he'd have been dead hours ago if it were. Anyway, the fact that the temperature out here had to be minus forty degrees should help thicken his blood, or slow it down if it was running out.

He wasn't an expert on blood clotting, but it made sense to him. And he was the only one he had to convince.

Leaving a trail of blood was his chief concern now, other than the pain. And not because the Russians might find it. No one would be out in this weather, and even if they were on his trail, the snow would fill in nearly as fast as he could crawl in this wind. It wasn't the Russians he was worried about. It was the very good chance that a pack of arctic wolves might pick up the scent of his blood. Once they found it they'd follow it through any kind of weather.

Avalik adjusted his goggles and glanced up over the mogul. Snow and blowing snow and darkness beyond. It was an exertion even to breathe. He pulled himself forward, digging handholds in the crusty snow and moving in steady lurches. I'm not going to be a late-night snack for some band of goddamn maurading wolves, he told himself. Not this goddamn Eskimo.

He moved an arm's length at a time, oblivious to the cold. In twelve hours he figured he'd crawled about a mile and a half from Jones's Strip. It was eleven miles from Jones's cabin to the base camp. They'd find him. He knew that. But they were going to find him alive. *Somebody* had to tell them about the fucking Russians.

Caffey dumped a wastebasket brimming with papers into a large cardboard box. Then another. He'd been at this for two hours. Lt. Col. Klugen, the previous deputy brigade commander, obviously didn't know what it meant to update files. His office filing system was a disaster. That would change, Caffey decided, immediately.

The office itself wasn't particularly large and the furniture was gray metal stuff that had been liberated from a Navy vessel (the inside drawers were stamped U.S.S. EAGLETON). Without any windows to interrupt the surface of the walls, Klugen had stuck up maps and charts and notices with tape. All that remained were yellowed corners of paper attached to pieces of tape and one large map of Alaska with a tiny American flag and the colors of the 171st pinned over Fairbanks. To one side of the desk had been a standard-sized American flag that stank of cigar smoke. It was in the trash carton as well.

Caffey was nearly through all the desk drawers when someone entered. He was a tall black man with captain's bars on his lapels. He was also chewing a doughnut and, by his expression, surprised to find anyone in the office.

"Don't you knock, Captain?" Caffey said. He was in his shirtsleeves and had worked up a slight sweat.

"Colonel Caffey?" The captain held the doughnut just below his mouth as if he'd been suddenly frozen in prelude to the act of biting.

"That's the name on the door. Who might you be?"

"Ah . . ." He brought the doughnut down quickly, eventually hiding it out of sight behind his back. "Captain Devery, sir. Captain George Devery. Brigade adjutant." He smiled weakly. "You're a little early, Colonel. I mean, I didn't expect to see you—"

"I opened up the place this morning."

"Oh. When was that, sir."

"Oh-five-thirty."

Devery's eyes got wide.

"Don't worry, Captain. It won't be a regular schedule. I just wanted to get down here and see what sort of office I was inheriting." Caffey gestured at the boxes of trash. "As you can see, I'd like a few things eliminated."

Devery stood straighter. "Yes, sir."

"Just calm yourself, Devery. I'm not head-hunting. Sit down. Finish your doughnut." Devery obeyed. He held the pastry in front of him but didn't bite into it. "Is that a 101st patch you're wearing?"

"Yes, sir."

"Do you miss it?"

"Sir?"

Caffey flew his hand in the air. "Whoosing a chopper around."

"Oh, hell no . . . I mean, it's safer on the ground."

Caffey nodded. He searched for something on his desk. "Now, George, there are some other loose ends I'd like to get straightened out." He found some pages clipped together and handed them over to Devery. "Did you mark these 'priority'?"

Devery glanced through the papers using one hand. He still held the doughnut in the other. "I believe I did, sir. Colonel Klugen left some things for you that he said were priority." He looked sheepishly at Caffey. "The deputy brigade commander has always handled matters like this."

"Well, then, let's handle them. I don't want to patronize this job, do I, George?"

"Ah, no, sir."

"Priority number one," Caffey said, holding a memo before him and reading from it, "'To executive officer acting as DBC'—me—" he said "'reply necessary in response to correspondence from Mrs. M. Burrows 7/23, 8/5, 8/19, 8/28 and 10/8. Information concerning the welfare of her son, Bernard A. Burrows, E-Three, Private First Class, Platoon eight, 171st Infantry Brigade. Request for explanation of her son's lack of letter-writing.' Etcetera, etcetera. 'Please investigate.'" He looked at Devery. "Have we investigated?"

"Yes, sir."

"And?"

"As far as we can determine, Colonel, there doesn't seem to be any E-Three Private First Class Bernard A. Burrows in the 171st Infantry Brigade . . . or the 172nd, or the 22nd Aviation Battalion."

"Have you tried the Coast Guard?"

"Oh, no, sir. I didn't think—"

"Order of the day, Captain," Caffey interrupted. "Find Burrows at any cost."

"Yes, sir." Devery nodded as if he were making a special mental note. "Colonel, ah, we *do* have a Bernie Burrows . . . no middle initial."

Caffey looked at him incredulously. "What?"

"He isn't an E-Three, sir. He's an E-Two. He's a clerk typist . . . works down the hall."

"Burrows? *Our* Burrows!"

"But no middle ini—"

*"I'll* give him an initial!" Caffey stomped to the door.

"Some of the work here is more interesting, Col—"

"Burrows!" Caffey yelled into the hall. "Bernie Burrows, you sonofabitch, wherever you are! Write your mother—or I'll ship you to an ice floe on the Bering Strait!" He slammed the door and turned to Devery. "Now, Captain, what other priority work have we to do?"

The call Caffey expected came less than an hour later. It was General Roberts, and he wasn't happy. "Caffey, get over here on the double!"

Caffey didn't have time to reply because the line disconnected.

"I'll be in the general's office," he said to Devery as he passed the captain's office. He walked slowly, adjusting his tie. Roberts wanted efficiency and no initiative, that's what he got.

Roberts's office was three times the size of Caffey's. The walls were covered with unit citations, plaques, photographs and two enormous flags flanked his desk. The general was standing before a huge map, following some line with his finger. As Caffey entered, Roberts spun around in a rage.

"What the hell are you doing down there, Caffey?" he said. His face was slightly red. A large cigar was burning in his ashtray. "Jesus Christ, I just spoke to Major Davis in Records and he tells me you've requisitioned a complete file reverification. Personnel says you want an update on the survival training status of every man in the brigade. And my secretary said something about a lunatic hollering in the corridors for the head of"—he stopped to glance at a note on his desk—"a Private B. A. Burrows." He looked at Caffey with fire in his eyes. *"What the hell's going on!"*

"I'm not sure I understand," Caffey said. "Colonel Klugen left a list of items to be looked after by his replacement. Priority marked."

"That square-headed sonof—" Roberts shook his

head. "Never mind. Look, Colonel, I told you we had a smooth operation here. I don't want you or anyone else fucking it up. Understand?"

"Understood."

"Damn better be."

"Is that all, General?"

"No, goddamnit! I'll tell you when I'm finished." He took his cigar from the ashtray and puffed it several times until he'd produced a heavy cloud of smoke around his head. "We've got other problems." He walked to the map and jabbed a finger in the northwest section—the Philip Smith Mountains. "Here," Roberts said gruffly.

Caffey moved closer. "What's the problem?"

"We have a company on competitive maneuvers up there. Four National Guard squads were on a timed march and reconnaissance sweep of this area."

Caffey studied the map. "And?"

"Three squads returned to the fire base. One's missing."

"Any contact?"

"No. The weather is terrible up there. Communications are all screwed up. NORAD reported they lost one of their Dewline stations. They went down for repairs and were never heard from again. And nobody can get to them until this weather clears."

"A NORAD radar site," Caffey said to himself. He glanced over the map again. "How long has that squad been missing?"

"Last contact was 0600 yesterday."

"Is it an experienced squad of men?"

"They're Eskimos," Roberts said disgustedly. "They ought to know what the hell they're doing. Eskimos aren't supposed to *get* lost." He puffed on the cigar again. "The governor's been complaining that his National Guard is getting the roughest duty. This will make him *real* happy. I don't think they're missing at all, you know. Goddamn Eskimos. It's probably a screw-up between commands."

"Maybe." Caffey walked to the map. "How far is that NORAD station from where this squad was last heard from?"

"Sixty, seventy miles. Why?"

"Just wondering. I don't suppose they could have wandered up there?"

"In twenty-four hours?"

"No, I guess not."

"General Hooks called me," Roberts said. "He wants a senior officer to go up there and supervise the recovery of that squad. He wants someone to bring things together so we don't have the governor on our backs over this. He wants to maintain 'a good rapport' with the state of Alaska." He licked the end of the cigar, his eyes on Caffey. "I'm sending you."

"Me?" Caffey smiled and shook his head. "That's PR work, General. It's not exactly my line."

"Your line, Colonel, is what I tell you it is. Today it's looking for missing Eskimos and I expect you to handle this with your usual fervor."

"Look, General—"

"Go to that fire base and straighten this mess out," Roberts said, his voice rising. "That's an order, Colonel."

Caffey closed his mouth. He stared at his commanding officer.

"*Now* you can go, Caffey," Roberts said. He puffed his cigar. "Have a nice trip."

Fire Base Bravo was normally an hour and a half chopper ride from Wainwright, the pilot had explained. Today it was two and a half hours. He didn't have to explain why. The helicopter rocked violently as it maneuvered through the high wind. "Better hold on, Colonel," the pilot had yelled over his shoulder when they lifted off the pad, "there's just you and me in this old bucket. If you get knocked loose from your seat, you're on your own."

Caffey's knuckles were white and numb where he'd

held onto the nylon seat harness with a death grip for the entire trip.

The fire base consisted of a hundred National Guardsmen on rotating duty, four helicopters and a small encampment of tents within a tiny valley of the Philip Smith Range. The purpose of the camp was primarily for training in arctic survival. Why it was called Fire Base Bravo, nobody knew. It was the only one in the northeast quadrant and there wasn't a Fire Base Alpha in the state. That was all Caffey knew about the place, but it was enough. He didn't plan on being here any longer than necessary.

"Colonel Caffey, I'm Captain Cordobes, company commander," said the tough-looking Hispanic who greeted him in the reinforced headquarters tent.

"This is Lieutenant Ed Speck, exec, and that's Staff Sergeant Johnny Parsons. Johnny really runs things around here, Colonel. The rest of us just come and go."

They were young, Caffey noted. Cordobes couldn't be more than thirty. Speck didn't look like he'd even started shaving yet. Parsons was the old hand. He looked to be in his late thirties, but it wasn't easy to tell. He was Eskimo.

"Morning, gentlemen," Caffey began. "I was hoping you'd have found our wandering squad by the time I showed up. No such luck, eh?"

Cordobes shifted his weight. "We were told not to send another patrol out until you arrived, Colonel."

"What?"

"General Roberts's orders."

"Why, that sil—"

"We've been ready to go for three hours," Cordobes said. He looked Caffey straight in the eye. "Do you think *you're* ready, sir?"

The lieutenant cleared his throat noisily. "Ah, sir, what the captain means—"

"I know what he means, Lieutenant." Caffey nodded to himself. "He's pissed. He's entitled." He looked at the captain. "I'm sorry about the waste of time, Cordobes. General Roberts is . . ." He shrugged. "He's a general. You've heard of the Peter Principle?"

Cordobes nodded. "Yes, sir."

"Whoever thought that up served under General Gard Roberts."

Cordobes smiled. "Yes, sir."

"Now that we have that cleared up . . ." Caffey pulled a zoned map of the Philip Smith Range from his pocket. "Would you gentlemen care to show me where the hell we are and what the best way is to find those missing soldiers?"

The best way was in a snowcat, Caffey learned. The last position the squad had radioed from was two miles west of a place called Jones's Strip, an infrequently used runway where a retired couple from upper Michigan lived. For whatever reason there hadn't been contact since yesterday morning with either the squad or Arnold Jones. It was the weather, the lieutenant had said. There were massive mineral deposits all over these mountains and somehow during storms radio communications went haywire. It was something to do with the electromagnetic waves, but he didn't know the correct name for it. So, the only way to talk to Jones or know about the area between Fire Base Bravo and the Strip was to go there. And the only way to do that, in this weather, was by snowcat, a monstrous-looking vehicle with snow tracks for wheels and a powerful engine that could propel it over nearly any obstacle.

The snowcat carried three passengers besides the driver and could pull up to ten men on skis. Caffey couldn't ski, so he sat beside Parsons, who drove. The men outside, five each on two tethers, were fanned out behind the vehicle in a wide V. If the squad hadn't strayed too far off course, they should run across them. The most likely explanation, of course, was that the men had decided to remain at Jones's place and couldn't radio base to let them know.

But all bets were off after two hours of searching. The squad hadn't stayed at Jones's place for the last twenty-six hours and they weren't lost. That was plain enough to Caffey even if nobody else had thought of it because, after two hours of circling through the snow, they found Corporal Paul Avalik. He'd been dead several hours and he was frozen stiff.

"Bled to death," Parsons said impassively. "He's got entry and exit wounds in his leg and right side. Somebody shot him."

Two soldiers had pulled the body into the makeshift cover of a tarpaulin lean-to beside the snowcat. They'd found him partially buried in a snowdrift. He'd been lying on his parka.

Cordobes was shaking his head. "I don't believe this. How did he get shot? Where's the rest of the squad?" He shook his head again. "Jesus, who'd shoot a soldier with a weapon in the middle of a blizzard? This doesn't make sense, Johnny."

"Did anyone find his weapon?" Caffey asked.

"We're still looking for it," Speck said.

"Won't find it." Parsons covered the dead man's face with a blanket. "Not in this storm."

Caffey looked at the Eskimo. "Sergeant Parsons, if a man were lost out in weather like this, for this long . . . would he go crazy?"

"Anyone else, maybe." He glanced up at Caffey. "But not an Eskimo. Not Avalik."

"Johnny, I have all the respect in the world for you and your people," Cordobes said quietly, "but the colonel has a point."

"No."

"Christ, he wasn't even wearing his parka! Does a rational man take off his parka in minus-forty-degree weather?"

Parsons didn't answer.

"Maybe," Caffey said, glancing around in the snow, "if he *knew* he were dying. Where is the corporal's parka?"

"In the snow where we found him," Speck said.

"Get it," Caffey said. "Quickly."

It was frozen inside out in a grotesque shape, the sleeves pointed outward and the back curved by the weight of Avalik's body. A pool of dried frozen blood was stuck to the hem and smears of blood were evident under patches of crusty snow on the back. Lieutenant Speck leaned the parka against the snowcat's tread.

"Oh, Jesus!" Cordobes said. He turned away.

"Brush the snow off," Caffey said.

"Sir, I . . ."

"It's only blood," Caffey said.

Speck brushed at it without enthusiasm. He'd taken most of the snow off when he realized what Caffey had guessed. "Sir, there's . . . there's something printed here!"

"Get a light on this," Caffey said.

"It's writing, but . . ." Speck stared at the colonel. "It isn't English, sir."

Sergeant Parsons's eyes got suddenly larger. He moved in closer, pushing the lieutenant out of the way.

"What is it, Sergeant?"

Parsons didn't answer.

"Sergeant, what—"

"Eskimo," Johnny Parsons said in a low voice.

"What does it say?" Caffey moved beside him. "Goddamn it, Sergeant, answer me!"

"Jones's Strip . . ." he said finally, ". . . all killed . . ." Parsons's eyes closed.

"Is that all?"

Parsons swallowed. He shook his head. "It says Jones's Strip—all dead—Russians."

Caffey looked up at Cordobes. His mouth gaped. "I want those men out there with fully loaded weapons, Captain," he said tersely. "Right now. Captain?"

"Russians?" Cordobes said stupidly. "Here?"

"Move your men out," Caffey commanded. "We're changing direction. Whatever attacked this squad is probably moving west along . . ." He looked to Parsons for help.

"Shublik Ridge," said the sergeant.

Caffey nodded. "Right. We're going to find out who did this and what kind of force they're moving. I want flank patrols and a two-man point. And I want it now, Captain."

Cordobes nodded. He looked stunned.

"And one other thing," Caffey said.

"Yes, sir."

"Until further notice, this company is the forward element of a combat reconnaissance patrol."

"*This* company?"

"Welcome to the 171st Brigade," Caffey said grimly.

They moved west, parallel to the ridge, under a gray, brooding sky. The wind had abated some, but it was still snowing. They'd established radio contact with Fire Base Bravo, which surprised everyone but Caffey. There wasn't anything wrong with the communications around here. The squad hadn't answered because there wasn't a squad. Jones was dead, too, if you believed Avalik's dying message, and Caffey did. Which is why he kept radio traffic routine and to a minimum. He didn't know who else was listening, and the fewer people who knew where he was, the better he felt. There might still be some other explanation for all this and Caffey clung to that hope, but he wasn't encouraged. He didn't believe in coincidences, and there was still a NORAD radar station suddenly dropping off the line to explain.

The men were spread out in staggered sweep formation with a scout at the top of the ridge. They were a pathetic little group, Caffey thought, fourteen National Guardsmen with no combat experience and an unarmored vehicle that couldn't stop a round from five hundred yards. They were boys, this little vanguard, dressed up like soldiers.

And against what? That was the sixty-four-dollar question. What were they up against? What kind of force was out here in this desert of snow?

Caffey stared out from the snowcat, scanning the rolling terrain for any sign of an enemy. He hadn't used that word with Cordobes or any of the men because it connoted a whole range of frightening possibilities, none of which he was prepared to deal with. Occasionally he'd notice his reflection in the glass—a man in white camouflage, snow goggles and a pair of binoculars hanging from his neck like some ridiculous caricature of Erwin Rommel.

"Colonel!" Lieutenant Speck lunged forward from his place behind Caffey in the snowcat, pointing ahead. A soldier was waving, motioning toward the ridge.

"I see him, Lieutenant." Caffey opened the door and climbed down from the cab. "Park this thing under a tree, Parsons, and turn off the engine. Then come with me." He jogged toward the ridge where Cordobes was sliding down in the snow.

"What've you got, Captain?"

Lieutenant Speck and Sergeant Parsons arrived a moment later.

Cordobes lowered his goggles. He glanced at Speck, then Caffey. "You'd better have a look at this, Colonel."

"What is it?"

"I think you'd better have a look."

Caffey squinted up the ridge. "All right." He turned to Speck. "Get the men about twenty yards up this rise and spread them. Lock and load. No talking. No smoking. I don't want to see or hear anything when I look down here. Right?"

Speck saluted. "Yes, sir."

Caffey sighed. Now wasn't the time to explain that you don't salute in fire zones, or, at least, in unsecured areas. He turned back to Cordobes. "Let's go, Captain. You, too, Sergeant."

It was a struggle, getting up the ridge through the powdery, boot-deep snow. Near the crest the three men knelt into a crouch, then wound up on their bellies and inched along to the top. A brief swirl of wind kicked up snow in front of them. As it dissipated, Caffey had an unobstructed though fuzzy view of the valley below. It was a winding column of troops and vehicles, moving at an angle slightly away from Caffey's position.

"Holy shit!" Parsons whispered.

"I'm praying, Colonel," Cordobes said quietly, "that we are all having the same bad dream."

Caffey studied the distant column through his binoculars. "It's a nightmare, but it's no dream." He dug his elbows into the snow for better support of the binoculars. "I figure eight hundred cold-weather troops, battalion strength. About a dozen snowmobiles protecting the flanks. Four armored vehicles, tracked. Heavy machine guns, antipersonnel rocket-launchers, mortars . . . Christ!" He lowered the binoculars. "The sonofabitches are loaded for bear."

"Russians?" Cordobes asked, staring down the ridge.

"They're Soviet shock troops," Caffey said. "Pathfinders." He handed the captain the binoculars. "That lead vehicle is flying a brigade commander's whip flag, Ninth Soviet Army."

"That doesn't sound good, Colonel," Parsons said.

"Those are arctic airborne troops down there. Probably the best-trained in the entire Soviet Army."

"What the hell are they doing *here?*" Cordobes wanted to know.

Caffey stared after the column. "I don't know, Captain, but I don't think they're lost." He glanced at the Eskimo sergeant. "What would a strike force be doing in this barren part of the world, Parsons? What's up here that has any strategic value?"

"Just what you see, sir. Nothing. They might head north toward Prudhoe Bay, but—"

"*That* war party isn't here for any Arctic Ocean port," Caffey said. He slid back on his haunches. "C'mon, I've seen enough. Sergeant, you keep an eye on our friends. I have a telephone call to make."

"What are we going to *do?*" Cordobes said as they moved back down the ridge.

"I'm not sure, Captain," Caffey mumbled. "But we're *not* going to attack them."

An angry General Roberts entered the communications center biting a cigar. He was just leaving his office to go to lunch when he was called by Major Breckenridge to come to the radio room. Urgent, she said. Colonel Caffey had a Green Giant message. Green Giant was this month's code phrase for contact with hostile forces.

"What the hell is Caffey up to now?" Roberts ranted.

Kate looked up from the duty desk where she'd been making notes. She was obviously shaken. "Colonel Caffey's reported a major hostile force in the area of Shublik Ridge." She nodded at the message center operator who was translating the coded radio key transmission. "The text is coming in now."

"Hostile force? What goddamn hostile force?" He pulled the cigar out of his mouth. "I sent the sonofabitch to find ten missing Guardsmen and he calls back with hostile forces at Shublik Ridge? Christ Almighty, Major, what kind of training game is he trying to pull?"

She ripped the page out of the code translator as the operator finished and handed it to the general. "Read this."

Roberts's lips moved as he read quickly over the message.

"Jake Caffey may be a sonofabitch, General," Kate said evenly, "but he doesn't play games."

Roberts glanced at the major with a dumbfounded

expression, then looked back at the page. "Battalion-strength land force . . . heavily armed . . . tracked vehicles . . . Ninth Soviet Army . . ." He looked up at her. "Is he nuts?"

"I don't think—"

"Christ! Where is he?"

Kate pointed to a grease-penciled circle on the plastic map on the wall. "There."

"Right in the middle of goddamn nothing?" Roberts exploded. "Get Caffey on the horn, Corporal. I want to hear this from him."

"It isn't secure, General," Kate protested. "The radio isn't—"

"Neither is Colonel Caffey after this little drama."

"Campus Darkness to Gallant Entry," the radio operator said into his chest microphone. "Campus Darkness to Gallant Entry." After a moment the operator looked up at the general. "I have Gallant Entry Six, sir."

Roberts took the microphone and switched on the speaker. "Six, this is One. Do you copy?" The general waited as the speaker rattled static, then—

"This is Gallant Entry Six." It was Caffey's voice. He sounded impatient. "Did you copy coded message? Over."

"I send you out to cover a situation that a retarded recruit could handle and you call back with Green Giants? Look, you idiot, don't start playing training games with this command! I'm in charge here and *I'll* let you know when I want to exercise an alert drill. Is that clear, mister?"

"It isn't a drill," the voice said tinnily from the speaker. "Over."

Roberts bared his teeth at Kate. "The sonofabitch wants a court-martial," he hissed.

Kate glanced up from the message. "He says the squad they were looking for was wiped out, General."

"It also says they only found one body."

"One or fifty-one, General, Caffey wouldn't make it up—not even for a drill."

"Shit!" To Caffey, Roberts said, "Are you under fire?"

"No," was the quick response. "This is not a secure net, Campus Darkness."

"Have you made any contact at all?"

"An observation only."

"Confirmed?"

There was a momentary silence from the speaker. "How would you like me to confirm it, One? Do you want to speak to them?"

"Insolent bastard," Roberts said.

Kate moved beside the general. "Sir, I'd suggest Caffey and his men continue to track whatever they've found until we can verify who it really is from this end."

The general chewed on it a moment. "Right," he said finally. "Caf—er, Six, carry on."

"Say again?"

"I said, carry on . . . carry on! Continue observation but do not engage. Repeat, do not engage. Wait for my next transmission. Copy?"

"Roger, copy. Gallant Entry, out."

Roberts tossed the microphone back to the operator. "Corporal, you didn't hear that transmission, so don't repeat it. I don't want a rumor started in this command that we're being invaded by a phantom battalion of the goddamn Soviet Army. Understand?"

The radio operator nodded nervously. "Yes, *sir*."

Roberts turned to Kate. "Major Breckenridge, I want you to get Division and tell them that the deputy brigade commander reported an unidentified force from the field. Tell them everything he told us *except* that business about the Ninth Soviet Army. I don't want to look like a goddamn fool."

"But—"

"*Then,* Major, get Captain Devery and deliver him to my office. I want a chopper ready in twenty minutes. We're going up there."

"But the weather," Kate said. "It's getting worse, General."

"Screw the goddamn weather."

"But Colonel Caffey is waiting to hear from you, sir."

"He'll hear from me all right," Roberts said. "Personally." He stuffed the unlit cigar into his mouth and stomped out.

Kate sighed and shook her head. "Jesus," she said softly.

Caffey jumped down from the rear of the snowcat. Captain Cordobes was waiting. "Well, Colonel? Did you get an acknowledgment?"

Caffey nodded his head in disgust. "Yeah."

"So, what do we do?"

"We track and observe until General Roberts decides what *he* wants to do."

"Are they sending reinforcements?"

Caffey glanced at the sky. "He didn't say."

"But, sir, we can't watch them indefinitely. They're bound to see sooner or later."

"Not if we play our cards right, which is exactly what I intend to do, Captain."

"But—"

"Assemble the men, Cordobes."

"You're not going to *tell* them, sir?"

"Yes, Captain, that's what I'm going to do. There are fourteen of us and eight hundred of them. I think they ought to know that."

"It'll scare the shit out of them," Cordobes said. He swallowed.

"I know it will. Soldiers follow orders better when they're scared shitless, Captain. And we can't afford any mistakes."

Cordobes nodded. He turned away slightly as a gust of wind blew snow in his face. He wiped a hand over his goggles. "Colonel, I . . . I think you should know. I've never been in a situation like this and—" He licked his lips despite the cold. "I'm scared, too, sir."

Caffey glanced up at the ridge where he'd posted the sergeant. "So am I," he said quietly. "So am I."

## PHILIP SMITH RANGE 1510 HRS
## 3 MILES WEST, JUNIPER CREEK

Colonel Alexander Vorashin's command vehicle slid to
a clanking stop a few feet from where another vehicle
had broken down. He climbed down and walked
around the icy gully where the crew was working
feverishly to replace a broken tread link. He scanned
the horizon. The snow was heavier now and visibility
was less than half a mile.

"How long?" Vorashin said to the vehicle commander.

"No more than seven minutes, comrade Colonel."

"It has been ten minutes already." Vorashin shook
his head. "If it isn't repaired in three, blow it up."

The officer looked at his men. "Yes, sir."

"If this column doesn't move, it dies."

"It will be repaired."

Vorashin climbed back into his command car. "The
driver of that vehicle should be replaced, Colonel,"
Major Saamaretz said from his seat behind the driver.

Vorashin motioned the driver to go on, then turned

back to the KGB man. Saamaretz was making notes in a small book. He'd been making notes all along, and the activity irritated Vorashin though he didn't mention it. Apparently that's what KGB men were good at. "Is that what you would do, Major?" Vorashin spoke without trying to hide his annoyance.

"Yes."

"It isn't the way *I* command my men, Major. It takes time to replace men. I have no time. Anyway, these are good men. The elements and unforeseen mechanical difficulties don't make them less reliable." He turned to face forward. "The vehicle will be repaired."

Outside, Major Devenko was exhorting the men, checking their equipment, moving them along. Vorashin unlatched his window, folded it down. "Sergei, hold the patrols closer in," he yelled against the wind. "Put five more men on forward reconnaisance."

The major raised a gloved hand in acknowledgment. "Done, already," he yelled back.

Vorashin smiled. "Are you cold, my old friend?"

Devenko blinked back in mock astonishment. *"Me,* sir? This is only a cloudy day at a Black Sea resort."

"Good, good." The strike force commander nodded approvingly. In a more authoritarian tone he said, "Check the front section of the guiders. I don't want any more breakdowns. Mobility is our best weapon."

"And the weather, Alex." Devenko glanced up. "Good weather for our mission. After six weeks of waiting, good weather."

The radio operator who sat in the back beside Major Saamaretz tapped his commander's shoulder. "The repairs to the disabled are completed, comrade Colonel," he said, holding the headphones back from his ear with his other hand.

"Good." Vorashin checked his watch. To Devenko he yelled, "We move. Inform all platoon leaders that I want five minutes back because of this delay."

Devenko waved and started toward the rear of the column. Vorashin put the window up.

"Five minutes?" Saamaretz said behind him. "You expect them to make up five minutes?"

"They'll give me back fifteen," Vorashin said. He turned slightly to see the KGB man from the corner of his eye. "These are *my* men, Major."

"Don't get *too* popular, Colonel. I—"

"Comrade Colonel," the radio operator interrupted. He quickly lifted the headphones from one ear. "Radar surveillance reports a single rotor aircraft in the vicinity . . . approximately six miles east, moving in this direction."

Vorashin opened his door. He stood on the running board, scanning the horizon to the east. He unlaced his hood, pulled it back and listened, squinting against the wind that blew his hair.

Devenko came running.

"Did you hear?" Vorashin asked.

"A helicopter." Devenko glanced in the direction that Vorashin was staring. "Perhaps it is only passing by," he yelled.

"In this?" Vorashin shook his head. He tightened the hood back around his face. "Any helicopter up in this area, in this weather, is not here by mistake." He signaled his driver to stop and jumped down from the vehicle. "Extend the flank patrols, Sergei. Split the left wing in two; leapfrog them every three-quarters of a mile. Post a reinforced platoon on the forward ridge to our eastern flank where they will remain and make contact if necessary." He'd been watching the ridge in the distance. As his glance moved to Devenko, his face was hard, unyielding. "Let us hope that our intelligence reports are correct, Major—that all we have to fear is a small company of untested militia."

"If it is an army division, comrade Colonel, we are ready." Devenko turned and ran back to his men, yelling instructions. The soldiers unaffected by the activity trudged silently on. Vorashin climbed back into his vehicle. He gave an anticipatory look to his radio operator.

"The aircraft is descending, Colonel," he said. "The air surveillance team is ready to launch."

"We wait," Vorashin said. "If the helicopter is here only accidentally, we will know soon enough."

"Why not fire?" Saamaretz asked anxiously. "If it is an enemy helicopter—"

"Because, Major, we must know where it is going," Vorashin replied as if he were speaking to a first-day recruit. "If there is a land force, we must know where and what its strength is. That is why. If such a force exists, the helicopter will show us."

"And if not?"

"*Then* it will be eliminated," Vorashin said quietly, "which should please you."

Saamaretz nodded. Then he opened his little book and made a note.

Caffey didn't have radar and he didn't know the chopper was coming until it was nearly on top of him. He'd been watching the column from a prone position under a tree. Through binoculars he saw the disabled vehicle being repaired and the tall man in arctic whites who'd stepped from the command car to inspect it. *He* was the leader of this little expedition, Caffey was convinced. He'd watched that man only and seen the activity as the commander stared directly at him from the vehicle's running board. Though there was no way he could have seen him at this distance, Caffey sensed the commander knew he was there. Then soldiers on the flanks began widening their patrols. The armored vehicle that had been disabled was now running with the others. There was something urgent in the way a platoon of Pathfinders broke away and double-timed toward the point. They couldn't have spotted his people, Caffey thought. They might be good, but they weren't that good.

"Colonel, something's coming," Sgt. Parsons said, tapping him on the shoulder.

Caffey heard it as he turned his binoculars back

toward the east. It was a low-flying Jet Ranger chopper, struggling against the wind, following the ridge line just above the trees.

"Oh, Jesus!" Caffey said incredulously, staring through the field glasses. "That's a brigade chopper from . . . My god! It's Roberts. It's goddamn General Roberts! The sonofabitch is giving us away!"

The chopper headed down, lights on, beating the snow into a frenzy as it settled in a clear patch near the snowcat. The noise was deafening.

"The stupid, shit-for-brains prick!" Caffey shouted into the blinding swirl of snow. He started down the ridge, half-running, half-sliding. Over his shoulder he yelled, "Spread the men at intervals, Captain! And for godsakes watch that fucking column!"

General Roberts was first out of the helicopter, followed quickly by two others, one of them Devery, all of them bent over, scurrying out from under the whining, decelerating rotor blade. Caffey reached them at the snowcat as they were dusting snow from their goggles and face masks. He directed his attention—his rage—toward Roberts. When he recognized Kate as one of the others his anger only increased.

"What are you doing here!" Caffey demanded loudly. He stood directly in front of Roberts. "You're not supposed to *be* here!"

"I came to see your invasion force," Roberts said matter-of-factly. He was wearing a yellow parka with his rank prominently sewn on the shoulders. "Where is it?"

"You almost landed on it, for Chrissakes!" Caffey glanced at Kate. "They didn't know *we* were here two minutes ago. Why didn't you just drop some flares while you—"

"You don't talk like that to me, Colonel!" Roberts exploded.

"Didn't you see it?—the column?"

"We didn't see a goddamn thing! Where *are* your Russians?"

Caffey pointed to the ridge. It was his second choice

of action. Punching General Roberts was the first. "You can see the column from up there. Did you bring any weapons?"

"Weapons?" Roberts stared back at him blankly.

"You came all the way out here without—" Caffey swore violently.

"Look, here, Colonel—"

"No, *you* look, General." Caffey handed him his binoculars. He nodded over his shoulder toward the ridge. "Up there."

They moved up the slope, Roberts in the lead. Kate struggled to keep up with Caffey. "Division's been informed," she said between pants. "I called them right after you talked to the general. I told them everything in your message. At least someone else with authority knows about this. I tried—"

"What the hell are *you* doing *here?*" Caffey said quickly. "Whose bright idea was that?"

"I'm chief of S-2," she shot back. "It's my job to be here, Colonel Caffey."

"Well, take a good look, Major, and pray it isn't your last one."

*"Ho-ly shit!"* General Roberts lowered the binoculars. He glanced at Caffey in astonishment, then scanned the column again with the glasses. "They're fucking Russian troops!"

"I told you that, General."

"But . . . Jesus Christ! How large did you say?"

"Battalion strength; eight, nine hundred infantry."

"I don't see any nukes," Roberts said.

"They have rocket launchers," Caffey said. "You can see the mounts on the second vehicle. If they have nukes, they have the launch platforms concealed. Those riggings won't support even the smallest Soviet nuke."

Roberts's eyes got wide. "I count six launchers. Jesus, they're loaded up!"

"They didn't come here to be surprised, General."

"Why didn't they use them on us? On the helicop-

ter?" The general handed back the binoculars and got
to his knees, supporting himself against a tree. "Maybe
they didn't see us, Colonel. Maybe they're not the
crack outfit you think they are. They probably didn't
fire because they didn't see us."

"I doubt that, sir."

"Goddamnit, Caffey, whose side are you on?"

"More likely they're waiting to see if we spotted
them. They *know* we're here, General. I suggest you
confirm the sighting on a direct link to TAC COM and
then"—he nodded down the slope at the helicopter—"I
think we should get the hell out of here."

Roberts glanced at Kate.

"I agree, General. We're not doing anyone any good
sitting on this ridge."

"Right," Roberts said. He motioned to Lieutenant
Speck. "Get on the radio. Get Wainwright pronto. Tell
them to patch through Fairbanks to TAC COM Pentagon, priority flash."

"Yes, sir."

"Tell them it's Greenstreet seven-niner and that we
have a confirmed Green Giant in—" He looked to
Kate.

"Alpha Echo Sector," she said.

"Alpha Echo Sector. You got that, Lieutenant?"

"Yes, sir." Speck swallowed, his eyes big as quarters.

"Then move, Lieutenant. *Move!*"

"Yes, *sir!*" Speck took off on a run down the slope.

"And get the men in the chopper," Caffey yelled
after him. He turned to Roberts. "C'mon, General."

"How the hell did they get in here?" Roberts said.
"That's what I'd like to know. How the *hell* did they get
through our first defense?"

"I don't know." Caffey motioned for the others to
move out. "We'd better move it, General. They've
probably got patrols out on the ridge."

"You think it was an airdrop, Colonel? You think
they just dropped in here?"

Caffey nodded impatiently. "That'd be my guess,

yes, sir. Probably coordinated with the weather . . . came in ahead of the front."

"But how?"

"I don't *know,* General. I expect it has something to do with that NORAD radar station going down. It's in the right area." Caffey slipped the binocular strap over his head. "C'mon. There's nothing else we can do here." Down the slope he heard the whine of the chopper's engine starting up.

"The sonofabitches!" Roberts was staring down the ridge at the column as it faded into the distant whiteness. "They'll pay for this." He got to his feet. "The sonofabitches will pay for this!"

"Don't stand up," Caffey yelled. "That parka is like a beacon—"

"We'll blast the bastards right back to hell," Roberts said at the top of his voice. "They can't just walk in here like this was goddamn Poland!"

"General—"

The sudden burst of gunfire exploded through the trees and cascaded an avalanche of snow from the pines onto Caffey's head. He fell backward, rolling several feet down the slope before he could stop himself. General Roberts lay facedown in the snow at the top of the ridge. His parka was shredded. The back of his hood was blown away from the exiting bullet.

Caffey scrambled down the slope, putting trees between him and the Soviet soldiers who kept up a barrage of fire from their positions farther up the ridge. Bullets splintered pine all around him. He dove behind the protection of a fallen tree and slid into Sgt. Parsons.

"Return fire!" Caffey screamed. "Return fire!"

Suddenly the ridge was a roar of gunfire. Snapped tree limbs and snow fell everywhere from the intense firepower. Caffey grabbed the M-16 and cartridge belt of a soldier who lay bleeding from a chest wound. "Move back," he yelled at Parsons and his men. "Move back to the snowcat!"

Then the slope was engulfed in a swirling snowstorm

as the helicopter's blade sang at full pitch. Caffey
dragged the screaming GI down the slope to the cat.
He'd lost his goggles on the ridge and he fought to see
against the missiles of snowflakes. The Soviets kept up
their fire, but they were also blinded by the driving
snow and couldn't pick targets to shoot at.

Caffey rested against the side of the snowcat. He
grabbed Parsons by the shoulder and screamed in his
face to make himself heard. "Get the men in the
chopper!"

"We're the only ones not in it!" the Eskimo sergeant
screamed back. "Where's the general?"

"Dead!" Caffey grabbed Parsons's hand and put it on
the wounded soldier's hood. "Get him in the chopper!"

"Okay!"

"Are the keys in the cat?" Caffey pointed at the
driver's door.

Parsons gave an exaggerated nod.

"Go!" Caffey yelled. "Take off in thirty seconds
whether I'm there or not."

"Colonel—"

"Go, goddamnit!"

Caffey pushed him toward the chopper. He opened
the snowcat door and swung himself into the driver's
seat, propping the door open with his rifle. He switched
on the ignition and pressed the starter. The diesel
engine turned, chugging for life. "Start, you fucking
beast!"

He pressed again and it caught with a sputter, then
roared. "Now . . . move!" He set the gear in low and
the cat lurched forward. Caffey swung it around in a
direction parallel to the ridge but toward the clearing
away from the chopper. He was guessing where the
clearing was. He couldn't see a damn thing.

He shifted into high, then pointed the M-16 out the
door in the general direction of where he thought the
Soviets were positioned and emptied the clip. Within
seconds they returned fire. Bullets pinged through the
cat's thin metal. The window splintered. Caffey
jammed the rifle between the seat and the steering

wheel and jumped clear. He was running as he hit the ground.

"Go!" Caffey screamed, scrambling at the side door of the chopper. "Go! Go! Keep below the ridge line! *GO!*"

Kate and Cordobes and Parsons pulled him in as the Jet Ranger lifted off the ground, swung west and accelerated. "Keep below the ridge line," Caffey yelled toward the cockpit. "The rockets can't track you below the ridge."

"He knows," Cordobes said.

"Where's Roberts?" Kate said. She helped Caffey sit up. "What happened—"

"He's dead."

"Are you su—"

"They blew his head off," Caffey said angrily. "Yes, I'm sure."

Suddenly there was an explosion behind them. A plume of black smoke rose from the tiny battlefield in the snow.

"What was that!" Cordobes said.

"Scratch one US Army snowcat." Caffey leaned back against the bulkhead. "I figured it was something they should shoot at instead of us. Helicopters are not known for their bulletproof characteristics." He glanced around him. The bay was crowded with soldiers, some tending to their wounded comrades, others just staring mutely out the open door. "What's the count?"

"Six wounded," Kate said. "Two are serious. The copilot was also hit above the ear. Almost blew his helmet off, but he'll be okay."

Caffey looked at Cordobes. "Where's Lieutenant Speck?"

The captain shook his head.

"Shit!"

"Ed did get the message off to TAC COM," Cordobes said. "Washington knows."

"Was there a response?"

The captain shrugged. "The bastard who killed Ed

Speck also destroyed his radio. He just had time to get an acknowledgment before . . ." He wiped a sleeve over his face. "What's going to happen now, Colonel?"

Caffey shook his head. He looked out at the blur of trees and snow as the helicopter rushed past them. "I don't know," he said finally. "I don't know. Washington will tell us something."

One of the soldiers beside Caffey leaned toward him. "Are we at war, sir?" he said in a low voice. He was barely twenty, Caffey thought. Someone else's blood was smeared across the front of his parka. "Are we, sir?"

"I hope not, son," Caffey said, looking away at the snow and ice below. "God, I hope not."

Col. Gen. Aleksey Rudenski was in the library of his home, sitting before an evening fire reading Chairman Gorny's redevelopment plan for the Central Committee, when the call came. Major Suloff was brief.

"We've received a signal from Section Nine, comrade General."

Rudenski set the report aside. "They are on schedule then?"

"One day earlier than anticipated."

"Excellent."

"They have made contact with a parallel group."

Rudenski frowned. "Yes?"

"Patrol strength. An observation unit only. An hour ago."

"I see. Then we can assume Washington has been informed?"

"Yes, comrade General. We expect they have been."

Rudenski nodded to himself. "Good, Major. Very good. Thank you for calling." He replaced the telephone and looked into the fire. "Now we see what the chairman is made of," he said softly. "Bull or lamb . . ."

# WHCR 1930 HRS

The White House Crisis Room was located in the subbasement of the presidential mansion, built in the days when it was believed crises were best handled deep underground, safe from atomic blasts and fallout. Crises were still discussed and argued there though, since the advent of relatively pinpoint-accurate megaton-hydrogen weapon systems, its effective life-supporting and safety characteristics were qualitatively reduced to those of a very deep tomb.

The Crisis Room was more than one room, of course, and it was staffed around the clock, generally with military communications specialists and NSC advisors, whether there was a current crisis to be resolved or not. The heart of the WHCR was the XCONSTRAT Room, an incomplete acronym for Executive Conference and Strategic Planning. XCONSTRAT was just what one might expect such a room to look like. It was large and had no windows and was illuminated by rows and rows of fluorescent lights. Its two main features were an enormous back-screen projection map on what was considered the "front" wall (the map could be made to show a flat version of the entire planet or any portion thereof, blown up) and a conference table with places for a dozen executive crisis-participants. Usually this room was unused; the back-screen projection map was off and the lights were out except when a security-cleared maid came in to polish the table.

Tonight the lights were on and the table was cluttered with styrofoam coffee cups, brimming ashtrays and Xerox copies of contingency planning reports in gray folders marked TOP SECRET. Present were members of the JCS—General Max Schriff, Army Chief of Staff; Admiral Vernon Blanchard, Chief of Naval Operations; and Air Force General Phillip Olafson, JCS Chairman. The nonmilitary executives present were CIA Director Burton Tankersley, Acting FBI Director Naomi Glass, Secretary of Defense Dr. Alan Tennant, Secretary of the Threats Committee Elizabeth Rawley and National Security Advisor Dr. Jules Farber.

Farber was the acknowledged chairman of the group, standing in for the president. They'd been here now well over two hours. The projected map on the screen was of northeast Alaska. A bright red marker had been placed at the location of a NORAD radar station that hadn't been heard from in almost two days, and a dotted line had been drawn to a spot understood to be Juniper Junction near a place called Shublik Ridge.

The men in uniform were in shirt-sleeves. The civilians had not even loosened a tie. Farber was speaking when the door opened and the president entered.

"Keep your seats, gentlemen," he said. "I'm sorry to take so long, Jules. I didn't want to cancel anything to give the press the idea that something urgent was brewing. The Cincinnati Boys Choir did two encores in the West Room and I couldn't get away sooner." He took his seat at the head of the table and glanced at the map. His demeanor changed immediately from social president to commander in chief. "So, what the hell have we got in Alaska, gentlemen? Trouble?"

"It's a special unit, Mr. President," Farber said, speaking for the group. "They apparently neutralized a NORAD radar station"—he indicated the spot on the map with a pointer—"here. It bought them a radar-free corridor for a Pathfinder drop . . . paratroopers. A large desant unit."

"Forgive me, Jules. You have to speak English. What's a desant unit?"

"In Soviet terms it's usually a battalion-strength force of elite troops designed to drop, clear, march and kill. They're fast, talented and . . . deadly."

McKenna nodded at the map. "And that's where they are?" He squinted to see the name. "Shublik Ridge?"

"That's where our people made contact with them," said General Schriff of the army. The four stars on his collar glittered in the artificial light. "It's the last known location of the unit. Assuming their rate of march is consistent and that Colonel Caffey's observation represents the entire unit, they should be approximately"— he stood and pointed out a spot on the map a few inches to the west of the last dotted line—"there."

"What I want to know, General," McKenna said with a smile, "is where the hell they're *going?*"

"We believe the intruding force will strike at one of three tactical positions within four days, Mr. President," said Secretary of Defense Tennant. "The civilian community of Stagwon, the ranger post at Mancha Creek or the pipeline at White Hill."

"There's nothing strategic about Stagwon unless they're out to get laid," said Tankersley of the CIA.

McKenna looked at General Schriff. "What about this ranger post?"

"It's nothing vital, Mr. President. Certainly not worth a strike force of this size."

"So, that leaves the pipeline," the president said. He looked around the table. "Right?"

"We haven't deduced any realistic motivation for a Soviet strike force to be marching on our Alaskan oil source, Mr. President," Farber said. He removed his glasses and rubbed at them with an enormous handkerchief. "None that we can agree on that is worth the risk, that is."

Defense Secretary Tennant said, "What would they do with it? There's no possible way they can use the pipeline short of siphoning off a few barrels. Anyway, if the Soviets needed oil their thrust would be in the Persian Gulf area—that's in their own backyard."

"Are we certain that these *are* Soviet troops?" McKenna asked. "From my daily briefings I've been advised of *no* indications of any Soviet preparation for a concerted military action." He looked down the table at Tankersley of the CIA. "Am I correct, Burt?"

Tankersley nodded bleakly without making direct eye contact with the president. "Yes, sir. Our Kremlin section has nothing to indicate any operation of this scale except some unusual troop movements in the Eastern Siberian area, but nothing that would support something like this."

"'No indications,'" the president repeated. He looked at the map again. "They have no backup units anywhere near the area, no capabilities for reinforcements, supply, or even to be withdrawn." He looked back at his advisors. "Gentlemen, as commander in chief of this country's military, I am not allowed to make mistakes. Not one. In order to deal with a situation like this I must have a few crucial facts on which to base some logical response. So, tell me"—he raised his voice so that it echoed in the room—"*who the hell are these people and what are they doing in my United States!*" He sat back in his chair and stared angrily down the table. "Jules, you have the floor."

"Despite the lack of 'indications,' Mr. President, I think we can reasonably assume that what we are dealing with is a Soviet strike force. Beside the fact that as a matter of policy we *expect* intrusions of this nature to be Soviet, in this case, I think, by simple elimination, we can deduce that they *are* Soviet."

"How exactly do you *deduce* that, Jules?"

Farber rubbed at his glasses again. "Who else *could* it be, Mr. President? We also mustn't dismiss Colonel Caffey's report. He *saw* them."

McKenna nodded. "How reliable is this colonel?" He looked at General Schriff.

"He's one of the best, Mr. President. He was just transferred in as deputy brigade commander from the 82nd Airborne, where he was training and tactical planning chief of staff. He's bright, aggressive and had combat experience in Vietnam as a company commander. I'd stake my reputation on his reliability."

"More than your reputation, I think," McKenna said. He raised a hand to cut off any reply. "All right. All right. They're Russians. I'm convinced. I just don't like to jump into a situation cold. You ought to know that the secretary of state has spoken to the Soviet ambassador. He was asked bluntly what a military unit of the Soviet Army was doing in *our* sovereign section of the Arctic Circle. Of course, he denied it. Comrade Orlavski is a great denier, which I can only assume is why he is the ambassador. But is he denying or lying or doesn't he know? Anyway, that's to inform you that State is involved in this now, too."

The president stood up. "I've been sitting all damn day. If you gentlemen don't mind, I'll just walk for a while. I think better on my feet." He grinned. "It gives my brain a rest." McKenna began pacing. "All right, then. Let's put this together. We've got about a thousand hostiles raising hell on our block. Therapy One. Send in a squadron of F-16s from Elmendorf and simply eliminate them." He glanced at General Olafson. "Phil? How bad *is* the weather up there for you?"

"*Too* bad, Mr. President. We can't get in there. That front has us blocked out like a sealed dome. I could send them, of course, but we'd never penetrate that weather. Fighter bombers, unfortunately, aren't effective weapons in the middle of a blizzard over extremely mountainous terrain."

"What about SAC?"

"B-52s are airplanes, too, Mr. President," Olafson said gloomily.

"So much for Therapy One," the president said. He turned to the army. "Therapy Two, Max. Ground troops."

"I can get a division to Seattle in forty-eight hours," Schriff said.

"That's fine, General, but I need them at Shublik Ridge—now."

The four-star commander shrugged. "I'm sorry, Mr. President. We face the same problem as General Olafson. With weather socked in like it is up there now, I couldn't get to them in less than a week. Maybe longer."

"What about paratroopers?" He gestured toward the map. "For godsakes, isn't that what those people are?"

"Yes, sir." Schriff licked his lips. "But they dropped at least two days ago, Mr. President—ahead of the front. We'd be jumping *into* that weather. And that's suicide . . . even *if* we could get a plane within thirty miles of that strike force, we don't have an airborne unit equipped for cold-weather jumps. Even if—"

McKenna held up his hand. "Thank you, General. I appreciate the problem." He turned to the chief of naval operations. "Admiral?"

"The Eighth Fleet is in the Caspian Sea, Mr. President," Admiral Blanchard said.

"Where it belongs," said the secretary of defense defensively.

"I'm satisfied that planes, troops and ships are where they belong, Alan. The trouble is I can't use them."

"We do have Polaris subs in the Bering Strait," the admiral offered.

The president glanced up and stared at him for several moments. "There hasn't been a hostile use of a nuclear weapon in thirty-eight years, Admiral," he began, "and if you think I'm going to launch a hydrogen warhead on the state of Alaska"—his face contorted in anger—*"from one of my own subma-rines . . ."*

"Mr. President, I didn't mean . . ."

McKenna calmed himself. "Of course not, General. I apologize for that." He took a long, heavy breath. "Well, then, we don't seem to have a lot of options, do we? For an intruder force that seems to have no purpose, they've thought this one out pretty well. The bottom line is that we can't get at them. Anyone care to disagree with that assessment?"

"Temporarily," General Olafson said hopefully. "This weather won't last for more than three days—four at the most."

"I have to assume *they* know that, General. So, now what?" The president looked at Farber, who was quietly cleaning his glasses. "Jules? I haven't heard anything lately from your corner."

"I think initiating a mass mobilization effort without calling attention to it would be proper."

"That would be a nice trick, Jules."

"No trick at all, Mr. President. Activate our ready reaction forces for a training and evaluation exercise. The Joint Chiefs do it often enough—to test reaction time. By notifying the Readiness Command at Tampa, alerting units of the 82nd from Bragg and the 9th Division from Lewis, swinging the Mediterranean Fleet around . . . we are mobilized without causing a big row. So, when conditions are right—"

"We'll have half a million men to do a job next week instead of half a division today?" McKenna finished.

"Or anything else that comes up, Mr. President. As you are aware, we don't know precisely what that Soviet force is *doing* up there. Maybe they're after the pipeline, maybe not."

"I *don't* think it's a surprise attack on Canada, Jules."

Farber placed the glasses over his face carefully. "Nor do I, Mr. President."

McKenna walked to the map. "Meanwhile, all I have

within striking distance of this elite corps of Soviet arctic paratroopers is less than a company of untried National Guardsmen commanded by a lieutenant colonel whose only combat experience was in the jungles and rice paddies of Southeast Asia." He turned on his heels. "I wonder, gentlemen, with a counterforce like that . . . how could we possibly lose?"

## JONES'S STRIP 2245 HRS

The landing strip was a scene of swirling confusion.
Night flares had been set out for the four helicopters as
they made alternate takeoffs and landings, discharging
soldiers and supplies, then returning in the worst of
weather to Fire Base Bravo for the rest of the company.
Caffey had been ordered to set up a forward CP at
Jones's Strip and to use every man available. He didn't
ask what his command post was to be forward of. He
knew there wasn't anyone else for two hundred miles
and there wouldn't be until the weather cleared.

Captain Cordobes and Sergeant Parsons were everywhere, running in and out of the LZ, ordering arrivals
into one of the two hangars for shelter, moving equipment, resetting flares, inventorying ammunition as it
was unloaded—all in the blistering night's cold. The
last chopper nearly flipped in a sudden heavy gust as it
blasted through the darkness toward the homemade
circle of fire, but the pilot righted the craft in time to
avoid disaster.

Jones's cabin was CP headquarters and it was busily

active with soldiers tramping in and out. Caffey and
Kate wore their parkas and stood behind the radio
operator as he tried to establish contact with Fairbanks,
which was to patch him directly through to the army
chief of staff in Washington. Caffey wasn't attached to
the 171st Infantry Brigade anymore and he hadn't been
since noon today. He was taking orders directly from
TAC COM—Pentagon. Once he thought how pleased
Nancy would have been.

"We found my scouts," Cordobes said as he kicked
his feet against the stone fireplace. He held up a
handful of identity tags.

"How many?" Caffey asked.

"All of them—nine. We also found Mr. and Mrs.
Jones."

"Where?"

"Shoveled neatly into a snowbank behind the Quonset hut. All of them together. Some of them were
almost cut in half by—" Cordobes glanced at Kate. "I
mean . . ."

"It's all right, Captain," she said. "I know what an
automatic weapon at close range can do to the human
body."

Cordobes nodded. He looked at Caffey. "Anyway,
Colonel, I figured we'd better leave them there until
someone can come and . . . you know."

"What about their weapons?"

"They didn't have any."

Caffey glanced at Kate. "They're pros, all right."

"I guess the Russians took them," said the captain.

"I guess," Caffey said.

The radio operator suddenly sat back in his chair.
"Holy shi-it!" He looked quickly up at Caffey. "Oh
I'm sorry, sir. I—" He pointed to the radio. "It's TAC
COM, sir. They say Orchid wants to speak to you.
Orchid is . . ."

"I know who it is, Sergeant." Caffey took the
headphones. "Go have a smoke, soldier."

The radio operator untangled himself from the microphone cord. "Yes, sir." He got up from his place.

"Oh, sir, it's a secure net call. There'll be a two-second delay for the voice incoder/decoder between each transmission."

"Thank you, Sergeant." Caffey put the headphones on and sat in the operator's chair. He ripped off a new page from the pad in front of him and found a pencil. "This is Gallant Entry Six, over."

"Lieutenant Colonel Jacob Caffey?" The familiar voice sounded a very long way away. "This is the president speaking. Do you hear me all right?"

"Yes, sir. Loud and clear, sir. Over." He wrote MCKENNA in block letters on the pad. He heard Cordobes's intake of breath.

"Caffey, I don't have time to learn correct radio procedure or worry about who is listening in here, if anyone can. Just bear with me. I have to talk to you straight and I'd appreciate it if you'd do the same. Okay?"

"Yes, sir."

"First, what is the accurate head count up there?"

Caffey took the clipboard Kate was holding. "Ninety-three warm bodies. Five officers. Thirteen NCOs. All the rest are part-timers, sir. Guardsmen."

"They're full-timers now, Colonel. They've just been federalized. You can break the news to them."

"I already have."

"Good." There was a brief pause. "How many men did you lose today, Colonel?"

"Four."

"Four?"

"Yes, sir."

"I'm sorry about General Roberts, Colonel."

"I'm sorry about all of them, sir."

"Yeah . . . you're right. That was dumb of me. Look, Caffey, I've got a hell of a dirty job for you and more of your people are going to die. They tell me down here that you're a tough cookie. They'd better be right because you're all we've got at the moment. Savvy?"

"I think I get the drift."

"The problem is, Colonel, that the Soviets have denied the incursion."

"Denied! They can't deny it!"

"Shut up and listen, Caffey. Of course they can deny it. Governments can do anything they like."

"There *is* a heavily armed Soviet task force out here, sir. You can believe that."

"They are not Soviets until I tell you they are. Do you understand that?

"No, sir. I *don't* understand it." He wrote FUCKING POLITICS! on the pad.

"What I'm trying to avoid, Caffey, is a war. Do you think you can understand that?"

"These are Russians, sir. They're *in* the United States. They've killed sixteen people that I know of, including the commanding general of this command, who had his brains blown out ten hours ago. I don't know what I'm supposed to think except to react to this as a definitely hostile action by a large, war-minded task force of very well-trained cold weather troops. I have a small unit here with four choppers and not much else, but these men are ready to fight if that's the dirty job you're referring to. I'm not a politician, Mr. President. I don't understand politics and I don't particularly like politicians. I'm a soldier. It's the career I chose. So, if you have something you'd like me to do, sir, I'd like to get started." Caffey took a long breath. He glanced up at Kate and Cordobes. Kate was smiling, shaking her head. The captain was white with astonishment.

"They told me you were a straight shooter, Caffey," the president said after a moment. "They didn't tell me you were articulate as well."

"I just try to do my job, sir."

"All right. They're heading for the pipeline, Colonel. At White Hill. I want you to do what you can to slow them up."

"How slow?"

"We don't want them to reach it before the weather breaks." There was a pause. "If you can peck at them,

punch and run, keep them off balance until that lousy
storm passes—I guarantee you a sky so full of F-16s
you'll swear it was a swarm of locusts."

"When does the weather break?"

"The best estimate I have is three more days."

"That's a lot of pecking, sir."

"Can you do it?"

Caffey scribbled on the pad. THREE DAYS. He stared
at it several seconds. "Ask me again Thursday, Mr.
President."

The officers and noncoms sat in chairs or leaned
against walls, each of them intent on the drawings
Caffey had made on the small blackboard he'd found in
the Joneses' kitchen. It had been a long briefing—
Caffey had had a lot to say—and no one interrupted.

"And that's it, in a nutshell, gentlemen," Caffey was
saying. "Each unit will have its own call sign. When I
call you you'd better be quick. All of us depend upon
each unit doing his assigned job. We're dead otherwise,
and I mean that literally. I don't care what you've been
taught before. If it doesn't agree with what I've outlined here it's because we're in a unique position. We
don't have any backup or support. We're in this alone
for the next seventy-two hours." He glanced around
the room. "Questions?"

A sergeant raised his hand.

"Go ahead."

"Colonel, sir, ah, why not just set up ahead and just
clobber the hell out of them when they come through a
gorge? We could blast them to pieces. Couldn't
we . . . I mean—"

"That's movie stuff, Sergeant. It doesn't work in real
combat. There's no way we can meet them in force
unless we want to give them one swift kick in the balls,
maul them pretty good and show a lot of flag and
muscle. But we'd only get one shot before they blew
our little asses away. We're outmanned and outgunned
eight or ten to one. Our one advantage is our mobility." He nodded toward the helicopters outside.

"There isn't time to give you the full course in tactical strategy against a superior force. We're not looking for one decisive battle. They'd eat our lunch. So, we avoid exposure to their flanks and leapfrog platoons with our birds, meet them sliding off their front and disengage before they bring up their heavy firepower. We'll drive them crazy, which means they'll have to be more cautious, move slower. And that's all we want."

"Can we do it, sir?" A lieutenant stood up at the back who was the company adjutant. "I mean, can we keep it up for three days? I don't mean to be disrespectful, sir. We all know of your reputation and we heard how you tricked that Russian patrol on the ridge with the snowmobile, but . . . well—"

"It looks good on paper but how will it work when real bullets are flying?" Caffey nodded. "I understand, Lieutenant. I won't try to minimize the risks or feed you some bullshit about all of us getting home again. This is going to be one goddamn bitch of a game we're playing—tickling a dragon's tail. Men are going to die. You will see horrible death in combat. But fewer men will die if we do our jobs. That's a fact, gentlemen." He looked around the room again. "Anything else?"

"Ammunition," Kate whispered from the radio operator's seat.

"Right. We are low on everything and I mean everything. You're going to have to make every round count. Impress that on your platoons." Caffey picked up Cordobes's inventory log. "We have eighty-six M-16s, ten thousand rounds of ammunition, six 7.62-caliber machine guns mounted on the Hueys, one M-72 missile-launcher with twelve antitank rounds, six 45-caliber pistols and two thousand rounds, two hundred grenades and thirty thousand gallons of medium-octane fuel for the choppers." He glanced up from the page. "That's all. It has to last three days. Ten thousand rounds is not a hell of a lot when you remember we're supplying the Huey gunships from that stockpile. Tell your men to save their expended clips. When a man goes down his buddy is responsible for taking his rifle and cartridge belt. We don't leave any weapons behind."

"What about the buddy?" someone asked.

"We leave our dead," Caffey said grimly. "We get our wounded out, if possible."

The room was terribly quiet for several moments. A corporal sitting on the floor directly in front of Caffey cleared his throat. "Sir, some of us never saw a dead body before. How will we know if—"

"You'll know," Caffey said. He glanced across the faces in the room. "It's one of the first things you learn in combat."

## MOSCOW

Gorny was in a rage. He was in his "official" office, quickly thumbing through a thick folder detailing the size and disposition of units within the Soviet Army. He was standing before a large map that had been brought in by a pair of Soviet security officers and set up beside his desk. The map emphasized northeastern Siberia. A line of yellow-flagged pins marked off a route from the Chukchi Peninsula across the Bering Sea and ended in north Alaska.

Rudenski was also in the room, seated in a chair near the windows with a view of Red Square. Standing at attention directly in front of Gorny's desk was Major Konstantin Suloff, formerly attached to Moscow Center's military headquarters as a KGB aide. His hands were manacled in front of him.

"We have denied the unit exists!" Gorny was saying. He tore at the folder, searching. "If the unit does exist it is . . ."—he turned several more pages until he stopped—"it is the 22nd Infantry Brigade of the Far Eastern Military District." He looked up at Suloff.

"Comrade Chairman, we don't have a 22nd Infantry Brigade of the Far Eastern Military District. That unit was disbanded in 1979."

Gorny slammed the folder closed. "Damnit, Suloff! Perhaps it's the 19th Brigade, or the six hundredth! I can't follow the movements of an army of four million! But Intelligence—not your KGB—*my* Intelligence informs me that—"

"That the 51st Arctic Combat Brigade of the 9th Army has not reported back from special training maneuvers off the Chukchi Peninsula. From the base at Provideniya, to be specific."

"What *special* training maneuvers?"

"That unit has been assigned special task-force duties by the KGB, Section D, Detail 101."

"And Section D, Detail 101 is *whose* desk at the KGB?"

"It's my desk, comrade Chairman," Suloff answered calmly. "Which, I assume, is why you've sent for me."

Gorny gave Rudenski a look of astonishment. "He assumes? *Assumes!* He organizes a secret brigade, trains them for a special mission at a Siberian outpost, then airlifts them across a forbidden zone and drops them into the United States *and he assumes!*" Gorny turned and slapped his hand on his desk. "Does anyone understand what this idiot has done!" He stood in front of Suloff. "Do *you*, Major?"

Suloff remained silent.

The chairman walked around the desk and stood behind his chair. "For the first time since I was elected to this position, I am avoiding calls from the president of the United States. I have an ambassador in Washington half-crazy with confusion—frightened into a simpering mass of incoherent denials. He thinks he's been set up by me . . . deliberately kept out of this so he would appear to be telling the truth."

"It wouldn't be the first time, comrade Chairman," Suloff said softly.

"You are not only impertinent, Major, you are also

suicidal!" Gorny roared. "You won't live to see the war
you are trying to push me into! Do you understand?"

The major allowed a tiny smile.

"Get out!" Gorny shouted. He turned to the security
officers. "Take this lunatic away!"

When they were gone, he looked at Rudenski. "He is
insane, Aleksey. Do you realize that? Does he actually
believe his antiparty adventurism has any place—"

"I don't think comrade Suloff is insane," Rudenski
said. He rose from his seat and paused a moment
before the window. "The major is one of the most
dedicated patriots I have in the KGB. He—"

"He's invaded the United States of America!" the
chairman shot back bitterly. "I don't know what he
thinks he's plotting, General, but he will pay for it with
his life!"

Rudenski shook his head. "Comrade Chairman, it is
no counterrevolutionary plot, no nonsensical Trotsky-
ite brigandage." He turned to face Gorny. "We are
totally Marxist."

"We . . .?" The chairman's eyes opened wide. "My
God! *You're* behind this!"

"The time has come to face reality, comrade Chairman."

"You *are* insane!"

"Pragmatic," Rudenski said. "I prefer that. A lesser
observation would be incorrect and"—he raised an
eyebrow—"unwise, if I may say so, comrade Chairman."

"You threaten *me?*"

"I have a wide base of support, comrade."

"You have *no* support in the Central Committee."

"Comrade Chairman, you have less." He moved to
Gorny's desk and stared across it at the party chairman.
"The present actions or inactions of the Politburo are a
national disaster. We feel our initiatives"—he indicated
the map with a nod—"could revive the party."

"You speak of the party in the same breath as . . ."

"Look to the streets, comrade. It all started sixty-six
years ago in the streets. Have you forgotten? It started

in the streets with starving people clawing at walls with bleeding nails."

"I will not collaborate with insanity."

"And we will not collaborate with exhaustion and hunger. We'll not sit on lofty terraces drinking vodka and watching our country whimper itself back to the obscenity of starvation." Rudenski moved to the map. "In any event, comrade Chairman, President McKenna will hold *you* personally responsible for this. You might as well study our plan. You may find that it appeals to you. You may even claim it as your own. Even that would be in order, comrade."

Gorny gave him a sneering look. "Not possibly."

"Anything in this day and time is possible, comrade. Anything." He started for the door. "I will have the details of our plan delivered to you within the hour." At the door he turned back. His face was menacing in the subdued light. "They will *not* go to war over this, comrade Chairman. The Americans will make a great deal of noise, they will puff themselves up in righteous indignation, they will accuse us of many terrible things, but in the end they will not be stupid. Their generals will not act hastily because they realize that our generals are not insane. There will be no war. I assure you." Then he left.

Gorny sat at his desk. He stared at the framed photograph of his son for several moments, then withdrew the telegram he'd received from McKenna from a drawer. "Assure him," he said softly.

# PART TWO

## PHILIP SMITH RANGE
## DAWN

There had been a heavy layer of snow in the night. The bivouac area was littered with mounds of it where the men had struck their two-man tents, and piles of snow had collected over the shelters while they slept. Platoon leaders hurried about, giving instructions, forming up the column for the day's march. The wind was not so strong, Vorashin noticed as he strode toward Major Devenko, but it was still snowing. The major was sitting against the tracks on the lee side of the communications vehicle, eating tuna from a tin. He smiled as he saw his commander approach.

"Sergei, it is time to move. Have you posted the relief point?"

"*I* am commander of the relief point today," the major said, shoveling the last spoonful of tuna into his mouth. He wiped a sleeve across his face and stood up. "It will do me good to get away from the column, Alex—" He nodded toward the communications vehicle "—*and* from our comrade, Colonel Saamaretz. I do not like him much, Alex. He is disruptive. He talks too much to the men. He asks them if any are Christians."

"I'll take care of the colonel, Sergei."

Devenko nodded. He glanced at the sky. "The weather holds, still. That's good. I think we will have a good day's march today. The men are rested. We should make sixty miles before dark, my Colonel."

"Fifty will suit me," Vorashin said. "It is only ninety-five miles to our objective. I don't want to push the men too much. I want them alert and ready, not exhausted." He nodded to himself. "Fifty miles today will be enough as long as this weather holds."

The communications vehicle started up with a tremendous roar, and the two men moved away.

Vorashin gestured at the patrol that was returning from the point. They were on four snowmobiles, twelve men—four drivers pulling eight soldiers on skis. "Go, Sergei," Vorashin yelled above the engine noise. "And keep a sharp eye."

"For wolves and wild bears," the deputy commander said with a grin. "That is all we have to watch for, I think."

"Go."

Devenko waved. He joined his men as they began to fuel the snowmobiles. Vorashin started toward his command car.

That's when they hit.

A sudden, raking fire of automatic weapons cut down half the men in Devenko's patrol in the first few seconds. A snowmobile burst into flames. Exploding grenades showered chunks of snow and ice that thudded against the armored vehicles. Vorashin dove behind his command car. All around him men were running for cover. The wounded were screaming. Half a dozen men were already dead.

"Devenko!" Vorashin shouted. A bullet pinged against the metal undercarriage and slapped the snow beside his arm. "Devenko!" He crawled backward, inching his way to the other side of the vehicle. A

platoon leader ran to him, sliding to his knees behind the protection of the armor.

"An American patrol," the lieutenant yelled urgently. "Right forward flank!"

"How strong?" Vorashin could see platoons already
breaking away from the column, setting up defensive
positions on both flanks.

"Twenty . . . thirty infantry. Light automatic rifles,
grenades . . ."

Another grenade exploded twenty yards away. Vorashin and the lieutenant both ducked their heads from
the shower of debris.

"Move these vehicles!" Vorashin shouted. "Don't let
them sit here!"

"Yes, sir!"

"Send Twelfth Company forward! Neutralize
that—"

From the opposite direction, another barrage of
gunfire opened up. The lieutenant screamed as a bullet
pierced his forearm. Vorashin scrambled under the
vehicle, pulling the wounded officer with him.

"Bastards!" the colonel barked. *"Devenko!"* He
banged on the floor hatch of the communications van.

"I'm all right, sir." The lieutenant winced as he
rolled onto his side. "I will send the Twelfth immediately, comrade Colonel!" He pulled himself to the
trailing edge of the vehicle, got to his knees, then ran
for the cover of the rocket-launching craft.

"They came during the night!" Vorashin muttered
angrily. He banged on the hatch again. They set up
outside the perimeter and moved in this morning, he
realized. He should have extended the night flank
patrols, even though there was nothing in the vicinity
but an undermanned company of the regional militia.
He'd broken one of his own commandments: never
underestimate the tenacity of your adversary.

The hatch above his head opened and a sergeant,
armed with a pistol, poked his head down. "Colonel!"

"Get the vehicles moving!" Vorashin shouted. "All

of them! Now! Put the missile arms carrier in the lead
and order its commander to shoot anything in its path!
This column must move out of a crossfire!"

The sergeant nodded quickly. "Yes, sir!"

"Now, Sergeant, *NOW!*"

Vorashin crawled out from beneath the vehicle and
ran in a crouch to an icy gully, where a major was
directing a two-pronged counterattack over his hand
radio. Behind him, Vorashin heard the armored vehicles moving out. The rocket-launcher rumbled straight
for the first source of gunfire. It fired a missile that
exploded in the trees, directly above the Americans.

The major turned quickly to Vorashin. "They've
stopped firing, sir."

"Of course they've stopped," Vorashin said.
"They're falling back. They can't expect to sustain an
attack."

"Shall—"

"Keep after them!" Vorashin shouted. "Track them
down and finish it! We cannot let them regroup for
another skirmish!"

"Immediately, my Colonel."

"Have you seen Devenko?"

"No, I . . ."

"Direct your men! The Americans must not slide
away from us."

Vorashin searched the hills ahead through binoculars. There was nothing to see and he knew it. Whoever
commanded this militia of part-time soldiers was no
amateur. He knew how to employ inferior force tactics.
But he wouldn't get away, Vorashin thought. This was
a one-time incident, and rather suicidal at that. The
Amerian commander was both brave and foolish. He'd
hurt the column, but the damage wasn't crippling.
They'd be moving again in several hours. It was a
temporary hesitation and a costly lesson. If it were to
happen again, he'd be ready for it. But it wouldn't
happen again. The Americans would be tracked
through the snow and eliminated. It was that simple.

Vorashin jerked the field glasses back to the west

when he heard the distinctive thuup-thuup-thuup of slicing rotor blades.

The two Huey choppers rose over the distant ridge like a pair of deadly wasps. They swooped down side-by-side, barely off the frozen tundra, their fixed machine guns blazing, ripping through the middle of the column.

Bullets stitched a jagged line of divots through the snow. Vorashin dove to the bottom of the gully. He fell on his back, covering his head with his hands. He heard the major's death-shriek, and saw his chest turn suddenly crimson before he disappeared over the crest of the gully.

The gunships passes directly overhead—Vorashin saw the underside markings clearly—in an earsplitting scream of engine roar and machine-gun fire. They were heading directly for the missile carrier. Vorashin suddenly realized what the strategy was. The rocket-launcher was aimed in the wrong direction to protect itself. Vorashin was out of the gully instantly, running to the armored troop carrier.

"Open fire! Open fire! Alert the rocket-launcher!"

He jumped on the moving vehicle and found two of its gun team dead. He pulled one of the men off the fifty-caliber machine gun and began firing it himself. Tracer rounds stung the air in an arc after the two helicopters.

"They're after the rocket-launcher!" he screamed at the other gun crew. "Shoot them down! *Shoot them down!*"

Over the ridge ahead, Vorashin saw two more helicopters. They were moving slowly, keeping low, straining under heavy loads they were not designed to carry. It was the attack patrol, he realized. They were using the tiny gunships as troop carriers. He cursed violently. The American commander was a clever bastard. *And* he was escaping.

"Keep firing!" Vorashin yelled. "Keep firing!"

The heat of the fireball from the explosion of the first attack helicopter stung his face. He protected his eyes from the debris. When he glanced up again, he saw the burning wreckage hit the snow and break apart. The second helicopter was already fading into the distant horizon, trailing heavy black smoke. The attack was over, Vorashin thought. One helicopter destroyed, the other badly damaged. But they'd done their work. Vorashin's missile carrier was on fire. Men were clammering out from its hatches. A missle fired itself and zagged in a flat, winding trajectory, exploding harmlessly in the tundra half a mile away.

The colonel climbed down from the gun turret and stood silently, watching his men. They were crawling out of their defensive positions, checking the sky for hints of another attack, tending to the cries of the wounded. He counted a score of bodies scattered across the battlefield. Whisps of smoke swirled in the gusty wind.

"Alex! Alex!"

Vorashin turned quickly to see Major Devenko running toward him from the direction of the missile carrier. His forehead was bleeding.

"Alex, I—" he gasped for breath and knelt on one knee. "Where did they come from?"

"That isn't the question," Vorashin said. "Where did they go?" He leaned down to Devenko. "How badly are you—"

"It is nothing," Devenko said quickly. He touched the gash with his glove. "I was standing in the way of a slight explosion."

"See to it, Sergei. We must get the column moving again."

"Of course. I—" Devenko stopped when he saw Saamaretz approach.

"So, Colonel Vorashin," the KGB officer growled, "the small American detachment poses no significant threat!" He gestured around him. "What would they have done if they were not so threatening?"

"The responsibility is mine," the colonel said. "I underestimated."

Saamaretz stared at him as if he were waiting for

something more. Finally he said, "Is that all you have to say?"

"What would you like me to say, Major? It won't happen again?"

"It *can't* happen again! It shouldn't have happened at all!"

"Yes, but it did." Vorashin looked at Devenko. "Get that bandaged, Major. Then I want to see all platoon leaders . . . in ten minutes. We must salvage what we can and get this column moving again." He glanced at the sky. "They won't come back today."

"Come back!" Saamaretz was almost hoarse. "You don't think they'll come back?"

Vorashin looked at him calmly. "Of course."

"Then you must find *them* first. You must destroy them before they have a chance to regroup!"

"Which is exactly what he'd like us to do," Vorashin said. "He hasn't got the men or the equipment to stage a decisive battle. He knows we would destroy him. That's why he's resorted to this skirmish action—hit and run. Sting and fall back."

"He?" The KGB major looked puzzled. "Who is *he?*"

"The American commander who is leading that troublesome unit. My adversary."

"Then do it, Colonel. Destroy him!"

"And waste time chasing him across the Arctic Circle?" Vorashin shook his head. "No, Saamaretz. Our mission objective is White Hill. We will continue as planned."

"And let them hit us again?" Saamaretz had his little book out. "Do you plan to let them strike again?"

"I plan to let him try," the colonel said softly. "His advantage of surprise is now used." He glanced at the sky again. "He'll be back. Next time, *we* will be ready."

## THE WHITE HOUSE 1330 HRS
## TUESDAY DECEMBER 15

"Lost a satellite?" The president rose angrily from his desk. *"Lost* a satellite! Is *that* what he said?"

They were in the Oval Office, just the president, Jules Farber, Alan Tennant and Elizabeth Rawley, quietly taking notes. Farber had five minutes earlier returned from a meeting with the Soviet ambassador.

"That's what he said, Mr. President."

"And they're taking a risk like this to recover a *satellite?"* McKenna shook his head.

"Not just any satellite," said the secretary of defense. Alan Tennant shifted uncomfortably in his chair. "Perhaps it is so crucial to them that they can't afford for us to find it. We know, for instance, that they've been working on a particle-beam weapon—"

"Oh, for chrissake, Alan, there isn't any goddamn satellite! I know that. You know it. You'd think Orlavski would be too embarrassed to even say a thing like that." McKenna paced behind his desk. "I can't believe Gorny would risk war over a piece of hardware. *I* wouldn't."

"It's a stall," Farber said. He held his glasses up to the light, then took the handkerchief from his jacket pocket and proceeded to rub at the lenses. "Gorny is trying to buy time."

"For what? We *know* that they're headed for the pipeline. What we don't know is *why*." The president turned to Tennant. "Olafson was going to put some Phantoms up . . . to test the weather. Did he?"

Tennant nodded glumly. "Yes, sir. Two F-4s from Elmendorf. One crashed on takeoff. The other got his radar equipment jammed up in the weather. He . . . he hit a mountain thirty miles from the base."

McKenna closed his eyes. For several seconds he was silent. Finally, he said softly, "No more. No more suicide missions. We'll wait for the weather to clear."

"They might as well be on another planet, sir," Tennant said defensively. "We can't help Caffey and we can't touch *them*."

"I already *know* what I can't do, Alan."

Farber put his glasses back on his face. "Admiral Blanchard has been pushing for the use of his Polaris subs again."

"You know what my response to that is, Jules."

"I promised him that I'd give you the pitch."

The president sighed. He stopped pacing and leaned against the back of his chair. "One minute," he said, glancing at his watch.

"The *Ulysses* is in the Bering," Farber began. "It's carrying prototype Tomahawk cruise missiles. He says the crew can rearm the missile with a low-grade nuke, move the sub under the ice to the Beaufort Sea where he'd be within 130 miles of the target."

"Which is *very* accurate, Mr. President," Tennant added. "A direct hit by the Tomahawk would wipe out the invading column in a single blow."

"Accurate? In that weather?" McKenna looked sternly at his secretary of defense. "And if it were a mile off, or even half a mile . . . ?"

"It's passed a battery of tests—"

"In subzero blizzards, Alan?" He shook his head.

"We have one small US Army unit up there at the moment to keep a check on them. What if the Tomahawk was off a tenth of a degree? I'm talking hundreds of yards here. What if it missed the Soviets and, 'in a single blow,' wiped out *our* team?" McKenna pushed himself away from the chair. He glanced at Farber. "You can tell the admiral thanks, Jules, but I'm not that desperate yet."

"There is also this from Tankersley's boys at Central Intelligence." Farber opened a file from his briefcase. "They've got a theory you should be aware of, Mr. President."

"Just what I need," said the president from the other side of the room. "Another theory."

"You *wanted* this briefing, Mr. President," Farber said, slightly annoyed. "'Three heads were better than nine,' I think you put it."

"All right, Jules. All right. What is Tankersley's theory?"

"That the Alaskan operation is merely a diversion from the main arena—Europe." Farber adjusted his glasses as he looked over the CIA contingency synopsis. "With a preoccupation in Alaska, the Soviets may be planning a sudden chemical or biological attack through the GDR. If they can take out West Germany without a nuclear strike, they can mount a massive propaganda campaign to the effect that they have once again saved Western Europe from a reemerging Nazi era and—"

"The CIA came up with *that?*"

Farber glanced up but said nothing.

"Gorny isn't going to mount an assault on Europe," McKenna said sarcastically. "Christ!"

"There's a second contingency theory, Mr. President." Farber turned to another page. "An OPEC suicide force—a joint effort on their part to mangle our pipeline. Kill our hopes for the North Slope oil and keep us bending our knees toward Mecca and the Persian Gulf."

"I can believe that some of the Arab crazies would

think up such a scheme," McKenna said dryly, "but I don't buy the Soviets going along. They have too much to lose. We are talking about the very real possibility of *war,* gentlemen." The president paced with his hands folded behind his back. "They didn't lose a satellite. They aren't there as a diversion and they aren't there as part of a damn OPEC-inspired plot to cripple our oil supply. We know they are Soviet troops. We know they're in Alaska and we know they're heading for our pipeline." He stopped abruptly and looked up. "Does anyone have any other ideas?"

Tennant shook his head silently.

Farber closed the file in his lap. "An idea, yes," he said.

"Well?"

"Food," said the National Security Council advisor as he rubbed at his glasses again.

"Food?"

"The embargo. Grain is a weapon, Mr. President. We're using it, at least, with the same effect. People are starving in the Soviet Union."

The president frowned. "Somehow I'm missing the connection, Jules. What has our oil got to do with their shortage of grain?"

"Blackmail," Farber said. He replaced the glasses on his face. "Consider Chairman Gorny's dilemma, Mr. President. He wants no part of a nuclear brawl with us. He cannot afford to see his country disintegrate because of famine—something we could do something about. He also doesn't need a KGB bullet in the back of his neck, which is a possibility if he doesn't do *something* to ease his country's crisis. So, he thinks, if we hold back our grain from him . . . he'll hold back *our* oil from us."

The president considered it several minutes, pacing back and forth across the Great Seal of the United States woven into the Oval Office rug.

"It's possible," McKenna said finally. "It *is* possible, isn't it?"

"It's an idea, Mr. President."

"Blackmail." McKenna shook his head. "But if that *is* the explanation . . . Christ, doesn't he realize he's flirting with war?"

"I think he's counting on our cool heads to prevail, Mr. President."

*"My* head, you mean."

Farber shrugged but said nothing.

McKenna walked to a window and stared out at the Rose Garden. "Alan, when do we expect that strike force will reach White Hill?"

"Colonel Caffey's team has hit them once already," Tennant offered. "It's slowed them—"

"When?"

Tennant gave Farber a sober look. "Forty-eight hours, give or take, Mr. President."

"And when will the weather let up?"

"We're not quite sure."

McKenna turned back to face them. "Then we have forty-eight hours to work out something before that strike force reaches White Hill and our pipeline . . . which will necessitate a very grim confrontation."

"Yes, sir, that's what it looks like."

The president nodded. "Let's pray to God Lieutenant Colonel Caffey is the genius they say he is . . . or that the weather breaks." He looked at his National Security Council advisor.

"Amen," Farber said.

## JONES'S STRIP 1700 HRS

One of the hangars had been cannibalized to repair and insulate the other. It wasn't a beautiful job, but all it had to do was retain a reasonable amount of heat, which it accomplished, barely. But Caffey's primary problem wasn't keeping the men warm. His problem was keeping enough of them alive after each contact with the enemy (he was using the word now openly) so they could fight again. And again. Until he'd run out of men or ammunition, or until the Soviets quit and went home.

And they weren't quitting.

They'd keep it up, Caffey told one of his NCOs in response to a question during debriefing earlier, if they had to resort to throwing rocks and iceballs. Which was exactly what they'd be down to if later contacts were as costly as the first had been.

He knew he'd hurt the strike force. He'd killed or wounded probably thirty men and crippled if not destroyed the rocket-launching vehicle. Maybe they could patch it up. It didn't matter. It would cost them time. They'd be much more cautious now. They'd move slower. But the price he'd paid was staggering. Two of his four choppers were out of action—half his air force. He'd lost two pilots in the Huey that went down plus two thousand rounds of precious ammunition. A pilot in the second attack Huey was badly wounded and the chopper itself was no longer useful—the bullet-riddled fuselage attested to the miracle that it had returned at all. He'd lost nine men in his infantry—two killed, seven wounded. It wasn't a terribly high casualty count until you considered that he'd only used thirty men in the first skirmish; that's as many as he could cram into two choppers. Thirty percent casualties against three or four percent for his enemy weren't terrific statistics, no matter what he'd accomplished. He'd irritated them and that's about all he'd done. They weren't stopped and they weren't turning back. What they were was angry, Caffey thought. And waiting eagerly for the next time.

These were the things he'd explained in tonight's briefing. He took a long breath when he asked for questions.

"Sir, nobody's mentioned it, but . . . what about our families?" It was the lieutenant who'd asked if the plan would work the day before. "I know it sounds irrele-vant, considering what's happening up here, but some of us were due to go home two days ago. I don't want to go back until we've done our jobs, and I know our families don't know what we're actually doing, but . . . what do they *think* we're doing here?"

"They've been told exactly the truth, Lieutenant." Caffey offered a tiny smile. "You've been snowed in by the weather . . . and you're all eating well and getting exercise."

There was some laughter.

"How much longer can we keep it up, sir?"

"Until the weather breaks," Caffey said. "Until we run out of ammo or the people to use it."

The laughter died away.

"We did well this morning. But it wasn't enough. We'll do it again and again. We'll keep on giving them hell until we get some support . . . and I honestly don't know when that will be. The enemy knows we're here now and they know we'll be back. We kicked them in the ass and hurt their pride. The next time around it won't be so easy. They'll be watching for us. And our supplies are not unlimited, as you know. We have less than we had yesterday and more than we'll have tomorrow. We can't fight them and we can't ignore them and I don't think they're going to surrender to us, so we have to be smarter. And quicker. And more deadly. We also have a serious handicap in that we're down to two choppers. That means we use one for transport and one to cover our withdrawal." Caffey glanced at the chief pilot. "That means strafing attacks on the column are out. Their firepower is too concentrated. But at least we shouldn't have to contend with their rocket-launcher. That's a plus for our side. Another plus is they'll be stopping earlier to set up camp so they can put out perimeter patrols. That works for us for two reasons: first, they'll be forced to use more men in a round-the-clock perimeter guard, which means they'll get tired from being so alert; and, second, because we're not going to hit them at night. We'll set up ambushes farther down the trail, then hightail it out. We're not exactly the Muhammed Ali in this situation, but we will float like a butterfly and sting like a bee." He clipped a map over the blackboard. "Sergeant Parsons knows this area better than any man present. He's also the only one among you with extensive combat time. If there are no objections, I'm making him my XO in the field." Caffey glanced at Cordobes. "Captain?"

"None from me, sir. Johnny ran things pretty much anyway."

Caffey nodded. "Good." He turned to the Eskimo. "Sergeant Parsons, with the authority vested in me, etcetera, etcetera, I hereby grant you a field commission as lieutenant in the United States Army. Yo now an officer and a gentleman, which means you can use the officer's latrine without asking permission."

Several of the NCOs cheered.

Parsons stood and waved his charges into obedient silence.

"All right, Sa—Lieutenant. Let's strategize." Caffey pointed at the map. "Given the best conditions and figuring that our friends don't have another breakdown, find me the best spot to locate a choke-point ambush that's at least five miles forward of"—he pointed to a grease-penciled X on the map—"their present position."

Parsons studied the map several moments. The room was quiet except for the sound of the wind outside.

"I'd say here, sir." He pointed to a place marked Duggan's Fall. "It has good height to the west. They can't go around here—too steep for their vehicles—and on that side they've got a river. They won't risk equipment just to see if the ice'll hold." He nodded to himself. "I'd set up here, Colonel. They have to go through it."

Caffey drew a large circle around it. He glanced at the men. "Choke point, gentlemen. Our next offensive. We'll fly two platoons forward . . . here. Position our fire line . . . here, above them." He looked at Cordobes. "I'd like to lay in some fougasse, Captain."

"Sure. How much?"

"There are a couple of old snowmobiles in Jones's Quonset. I think they'll handle a pair of thirty-five-gallon drums each." He touched his fingers to the map. "I want them placed here and . . . here. Okay?"

"Yes, sir."

"And find the best marksman in the company."

"That'll be Private Cable, sir."

"Make sure he has the best rifle in the company."

"Cordobes nodded. "If I know Private Cable, sir, he best rifle."

glanced at Kate. "Major Breckenridge, what's ade and mortar count?"

"One hundred eighteen frag grenades, forty phosphorus. Thirteen mortar rounds."

"We'll need half the frags, all the phosphorus. I also
noticed Mrs. Jones had a pantry full of bottled preserves. We'll need the bell jars."

Kate frowned.

"If those boys out there are out a missile-carrier, it
doesn't mean they don't have portable heat-seekers. As
equipped as they are, they *have* to have Grail-type
missiles. I don't intend to lose any more choppers."

Kate's expression didn't change. "What do bell
jars—"

"Phosphorus burns hotter than any Huey engine,"
Caffey said. "If we have to, we'll make our own
antimissile system." He checked his watch. "Okay, it's
now 1750 hours. I want everyone assigned to this raid
to get five hours sleep. We'll move out at 0200 and be in
place by 0500. I figure next contact before noon tomorrow." He looked around the room. "Questions?"

No one even coughed.

"Right," Caffey said. "Move out."

# THE WHITE HOUSE 2015 HRS

Kimball poked his head into the Oval Office. The president was in his shirt-sleeves, sitting in one of the Victorian sofas that faced each other. Jules Farber sat opposite. Between them the coffee table was littered with Political Response Contingency Scenarios (PRCS) that the Secretary of State had drawn up.

"He's here, Mr. President," Kimball said.

McKenna got up and stretched. "God, I'm pooped." He rubbed his eyes. "Okay, Wayne. Ask the senator to make himself comfortable in the Truman Balcony. I'll just be a second."

Farber looked up. "Shall I . . ."

"No, no, Jules. You keep at it." He collected his coat from the back of a chair. "This shouldn't take long."

Senator Milton Frederick Weston rose from his seat when the president entered. He was slightly taller than McKenna, about ten years younger and, McKenna noticed with some surprise, his longish, tousled hair— the Weston trademark—was distinguished with flecks of silver. The one-time protégé was taking on age gracefully.

"Milt, it's good to see you." McKenna shook his hand warmly.

"Good evening, Mr. President," Weston said a bit stiltedly. "You're looking well."

"I try." He patted his stomach. "Dropped two pounds this week. Swimming twice a day. Did forty laps this afternoon." He gestured toward the chairs. "Sit down, Milt, sit down. How 'bout some tea?"

The senator sat down. "Thank you, no, Mr. President."

"I think we can dispense with the 'Mr. President' business," McKenna said amiably. "We've known each other too long to be politely formal."

Weston nodded without a smile. "I'm glad you could see me on such short notice."

"Anytime, you know that. As a matter of fact, I was about to watch a movie—Walter Matthau, Glenda Jackson, Ned Beatty. Spy stuff with a little humor. Interested?"

Weston looked perplexed. "You have time for movies?"

"Sure, why not. I can't be in the office around the clock. Even the president has to relax once in a while. Right?"

"I was under the impression—" The senator stopped. He eyed McKenna for a moment. "You're not trying to sandbag me, are you?"

"Sandbag?" The president gave him a puzzled glance. "It's only a movie, Milt."

"Please don't play games with me. I'm hearing rumors. That's why I asked to see you this evening. I want to get to the bottom of it."

"Everyone hears rumors in this town."

"This one is different. Something is going on. Something big that has everyone's mouth wired shut."

"Oh?"

Weston sat straighter in his chair. "What are you sitting on, Mr. President?"

McKenna sighed. "You mean, what am I sitting on *you* should know, Senator?"

"Not just me. The country. I'm not asking anything from you that is legally privileged. If you're sitting on a volcano, tell me. Let me help."

"*You* want to help *me?*" Weston nodded. "That's a change."

"You are my president. My party's leader . . . a mentor and . . . friend."

"In that order, I presume." McKenna's eyes narrowed. "Look, friend: Monday, Wednesday and Friday, you're my grateful protégé. The young senator whom I created. Antony to my aging Caesar. Tuesday, Thursday, Saturday, Sunday and holidays—holidays with big crowds—you slice me apart like a piece of third-class mail."

"You have great qualities, Tom," Weston said defensively. "You were a great governor, a superior senator, but, by and large, a disastrous president. I treat you as the occasion demands."

"And what does *this* occasion demand?"

"Tell me if there is a crisis."

"There's always a crisis in this town. Take your choice."

"You never used to stoop to sophistry. Something *is* going on, I know that. The Pentagon is shut up tight as a drum. The Joint Chiefs don't answer my calls . . . I'm not even sure that they're at the Pentagon. Tankersley's out of pocket in Virginia. Nobody knows where the secretary of defense is. And they tell me that Jules Farber has been hanging around here night and day for the last three days."

"Jules Farber hangs around here more than I do," McKenna said with a chuckle.

"*Are* you going to tell me?"

"I don't know what's got you all worked up. There is something, but it's not in the least bit sinister."

"What is it?"

The president shrugged. "I don't want to read about it in the morning papers, Milt."

"I don't leak."

"Of course not." McKenna nodded to himself. "As a matter of fact, the Joint Chiefs came to me to request an alert exercise. You know, one of those timed readiness tests. I'm sure the Pentagon is plugged up because they don't want to take the chance that someone will blow the surprise."

"Why come to you?" Weston asked suspiciously. "They can do that without your involvement."

"Money," McKenna said. "It's a loophole in the military appropriations budget." He sighed. "They *can* authorize a readiness test, but it comes out of their till. If *I* initiate the request, on the other hand, then the bill is routed through NSC funds. Olafson is pretty tight with a penny, you know. Anyway, I agreed. It's a favor I can collect on sometime in the future." He grinned. "See? No big deal."

Weston was silent for several seconds. "You're sure that's all? You're not keeping something else from me?"

"Like what?"

"If you're covering up something—"

"Look, Senator, I'm not about to kowtow to you or anybody else every time some silly rumor begs to be verified!"

"I'm just trying to help!"

"You could help by getting off my back. I have enough trouble with Congress and the press without you jumping in with both feet. If you *really* were a friend . . ."

Weston got up from his seat. "I don't want to keep you from your movie, Mr. President."

McKenna let out a heavy sigh. "Sure." He walked the senator to the door.

"I despise the people who steered me here," Weston said softly. He looked McKenna straight in the eyes. "But if I find that you weren't straightforward with me tonight, Tom, I'll hit you like you've never been hit before. You won't have a prayer for the nomination without my support."

"You really do want this job, don't you, Milt?"

"What I want is a strong republic with a strong president."

The president shook his head. He half-smiled. "I don't think you'd really like the White House, Senator. The presidency is *really* a job for a witty scoundrel, or a dummy with a brilliant wife. Not you. It's no job for the good or nervous."

"Good night, Mr. President."

"Good evening, Senator."

McKenna watched him leave until he was out of sight down the corridor. Then he closed the door and, after a moment's hesitation, headed back to the Oval Office. Farber was waiting.

It wasn't only Jules Farber, McKenna learned as he entered the Oval Office. Kenneth Quade, undersecretary of state, jumped to his feet when he saw the president. He was nervous, McKenna noticed immediately, which wasn't like Ken Quade.

"Mr. President."

"Evening, Ken," McKenna said. He glanced curiously at Farber. "What's up?"

"The undersecretary delivered a message," Farber said. He was holding Quade's brief.

"The secretary thought it would seem suspicious," Quade said. "I mean, if he came over here at this time of night. Your instructions were to maintain the normal routine. No cancellations of appointments. He's at a Christmas party for the Speaker—"

"I don't need details, Ken," McKenna said. "What's the message?"

"It's from Dimitri Gorny," Quade said quickly. "He . . . he wants a meeting, Mr. President. An urgent meeting, the message said."

The president raised his eyebrows. "A meeting?"

"A *secret* and urgent meeting," Farber said. He held up the brief for McKenna. "He would be very pleased to meet with you out of the public eye. He suggests Iceland. Reykjavik."

McKenna took the proffered brief.

"Within the next twenty-four hours," Farber added. He glanced at Quade, who swallowed. "He sounds serious."

The president read the message and handed it back to his national security advisor. He sat in the middle of the sofa and shook his head. "No, Jules, he sounds frightened."

## DUGGAN'S FALL 1145 HRS
## 62 MILES WEST OF WHITE HILL

Caffey strained to hear against the wind, squinting at
the white fog in the distance as if the exercise would
somehow help locate the column. He'd been here, on
this hill, in this prone position, for nearly seven hours—
waiting.

It wasn't a perfect choke point, but it was good. The
frozen river was to the north and the hill was to the
south. The column would pass between them, slowing
where the heavy vehicles would have to negotiate a
series of washboard-type moguls. That's when they'd
hit them, Caffey planned, when they were deep into the
choke point. The four fifty-five-gallon drums of fuel
had been buried at strategic spots and their tops
marked by small, twiggy pine trees to give the marksman an aiming reference. The men were dug in and the
choppers camouflaged with nonglossy white paint and
parked behind the hill for quick access. Everything was
ready. All they needed now was the column to show
up.

It's funny what a man allows himself to imagine, Caffey thought. Especially when his life and the lives of his men depend upon his making the right decision. Especially when he's sitting in the middle of a snowstorm silently waiting for a superior enemy to show itself. Caffey knew it was a good plan. He knew the enemy would have to come this way, but, still, doubts lingered at the edge of his judgment. What if they'd taken a different route? What if they'd split the column into halves or thirds and were at this moment flanking his position? What if didn't come for seven more hours? What if—

Caffey cleared the snow from his goggles. He changed his position in the snow slightly. They'd come this way, he told himself, and they wouldn't split their force. That wouldn't have been smart. Caffey was counting on that. He was counting on whoever was in charge of that strike force to be smart.

He heard the sound across the distant fog before Lieutenant Parsons nudged him. It grew into the distinct noise of small gasoline engines.

Snowmobiles.

It was the scout patrol, the point unit ahead of the main body. Then he saw them, the tiny machines skipping over the hard snow and out of the fog. Five snowmobiles each pulling four white clad figures on skis, semiautomatic weapons strapped across their backs. They drove into the heart of the choke point. And stopped.

Now's the time not to get nervous or trigger-happy, Caffey thought. He prayed the men followed his orders. No shooting, no matter what happens, until the flare. A misstep now and the whole ambush was lost. *We don't want the scout patrol. We want the main body. Hold your fire until you see the flare.*

He picked out the scout patrol leader through the binoculars. He was pointing north toward the river, then south toward the hill, then east. The men unlaced their skis and set out in pairs, weapons down and locked. Caffey wondered how many times they'd done this already today. And yesterday. There had been other prime spots along the route that might have been good choke points. A good point commander would have checked each one, which Caffey also counted on. There were better places for an ambush along the terrain the column had already covered since their initial contact. And at every place the scout patrol would check them out. The column would stop and wait until given the all-clear signal, then move again. It was the smart thing to do if you wanted to protect your men, but it was also time-consuming, dreary, tiring work. After thirty hours of it, men get sloppy; they get tired of searching and finding nothing, hour after hour. Which is why Caffey chose this place. It wasn't the perfect site for an ambush—the wooded hill wasn't strategically defensible—which the scout commander would recognize, but it was good enough because Caffey didn't plan to stage a battle here wherein he had to hold his position. He wasn't going to hold anything, just hit them hard and get the hell out.

The three pairs of scouts assigned to the hill didn't even come all the way to the crest. The wind swept snow in swirling gusts in their faces and it was plain they could barely see each other much less find Caffey's men in their spider holes.

It took the point patrol twenty minutes to join up again and another five minutes to get into their skis. They started up the snowmobiles and moved out, heading east, but left one team behind. That was the sign Caffey was waiting for. It meant the column would go through the choke point. The Soviet scouts were left to guide the vehicles through the least bumpy section of the pass.

Caffey waited fifteen minutes before he heard the first sounds of the main column. He aimed his binoculars at the sound and held his breath.

"There," Parsons whispered, nudging him. He pointed at a shadow emerging from the whiteness. "There they are!"

It was the command vehicle. Caffey recognized the pennant. He inched away from the crest. On his walkie-talkie he called to his marksman in a low, anxious voice. "Cable? Come in, Cable."

For several seconds there was no response, then: "This is Cable, sir." The private's voice was strained in the static. "They're coming, sir."

"Don't fire until they're in the choke point, Cable. You understand? Wait until they're all the way in. Right?"

"Yes, sir. Wait for the flare. I know."

"Good boy." Caffey turned to Parsons. He nodded toward the helicopters. "The moment the flare goes, I want those birds turning. We're not going to have a lot of time once the fireworks begin. I want to get the hell out—fast."

Parsons nodded. "They'll be ready."

"Good." Caffey pointed to a clump of trees about twenty feet away. "Take two men and the machine gun there for a—"

"Colonel! Colonel Caffey!" It was Captain Cordobes on the walkie-talkie. He was in a panic.

Caffey grabbed the radio. "For chrissakes, Captain, keep it down!" he whispered.

But the captain wouldn't be put off. Caffey looked up the hill about fifty yards away where Cordobes was pointing vigorously at the column. "Look, sir," the voice on the radio was saying urgently. "Look!"

Caffey and Parsons scrambled to the crest and looked down. The strike force was about half out of the fog, the vehicles leading the troops. *Four* vehicles.

"Oh, Jesus!" Caffey breathed. He grabbed the binoculars, quickly adjusting the focus as he trained on the third vehicle in the line. The sides were scorched black from the fire, it was missing its cold-weather shield and there was only one launch platform instead of four, but the missile carrier was intact, its single rocket bouncing on its mount and aimed in the general direction of Caffey's position.

"Shit!" Caffey pounded a gloved fist in the snow. "The sonofabitches fixed the carrier!"

"They couldn't have, sir. We—"

"There it goddamn is, Lieutenant!" Caffey snapped. "Shit!"

"What do we do?"

Caffey studied the column as it moved slowly toward his trap. "We pray the sonofabitch drives over one of those fuel drums," he said grimly. "That's what we do, Parsons. And pray Cable is as good a shot as he says he is."

Vorashin was out of his command vehicle, walking ahead of the column with the forward platoon. It had been a rotten day so far. Two of the wounded had died in the night and they'd buried them without ceremony before moving out at dawn. Also, the men's impatience was showing. There had been a fight this morning between a private and an NCO over some triviality. The NCO was now a private and the private was assigned permanent point duty. It was crucial to maintain discipline, Vorashin knew. From discipline came obedience and order. But it was difficult to maintain discipline when the rhythm of the march was constantly being interrupted. When the column was stopped, the men had time to complain. They were cold, or hungry, or tired, or bored . . . but Vorashin couldn't take the risk *not* to stop. Somewhere ahead, he knew, the American commander and his ragtag band of deadly zealots were waiting. They might be anywhere, even here. So the interruptions continued while the point patrol searched every possible ambush site for signs of a trap.

"Colonel Vorashin. Colonel Vorashin, wait a moment, please."

There was another problem he would have to deal with soon. Vorashin glanced over his shoulder to see Major Saamaretz hurrying toward him.

"Yes, Major. What is it?"

"I'd like to speak to you."

"So speak," Vorashin said. He continued walking. "I will listen."

"It's this pace," Saamaretz said impatiently. "We've traveled only eleven miles since dawn. We must move faster, Colonel. This moving and halting and moving and halting—it accomplishes nothing."

"We will reach our objective on time, Major. That's all that matters."

"I don't think the Americans are coming back, Colonel." Saamaretz skipped a step to keep up. "They haven't showed themselves since yesterday at dawn. I think it is because our soldiers proved that they cannot be intimidated. I think it is because the Americans haven't enough audacity to try another ambush. They know we outnumber them twenty to one. I think it is because—"

"It is because he is intelligent," Vorashin interrupted angrily. He stopped abruptly and Saamaretz nearly ran into him. "The American commander isn't a fool, my dear Major. He knows we must be cautious. He is planning on our slowed march to make his move. He'll come, Major. I promise you he will come."

"When?"

"Soon," Vorashin said. "Before dark."

"And we will continue this game?"

"What do *you* suggest, comrade Major?"

"It is your command," Saamaretz replied quickly. "I would not interfere with your judgment at this time. However . . ."

Vorashin glanced at him icily. "However, what?"

"This *is* a KGB mission, Colonel. You understand that. I am in constant communication with Colonel General Rudenski's headquarters. If at any moment comrade Rudenski becomes impatient with your actions . . ." The major shrugged. "You understand, Colonel, that you are only the military field commander. But this mission *can* be run without your direct control."

"Whenever you would like to take command, Major, you need only ask," Vorashin said quietly. "I have better—" The colonel stopped. He'd been scanning the path ahead, mentally searching for anything out of the ordinary. He had stopped so abruptly, near an arctic scrub bush, that Saamaretz hadn't noticed and had continued on several paces before realizing he was alone.

"Colonel, what—"

Vorashin ignored the major. He signaled to the platoon commander, who came running.

"Yes, sir?"

"Stop the column. Get Major Devenko up here immediately."

"At once," said the platoon commander and he was gone.

"What are you doing now?" Saamaretz asked.

Vorashin glanced toward the hill to his right. "You wanted to know where the Americans were?" He nodded at the hill. "They're here, Major."

"Here!" Saamaretz reached for his sidearm.

"Don't move, Major. If you want to live, don't move." Vorashin turned as Devenko approached at a trot. His forehead was bandaged under the goggles.

"Yes, Colonel?"

"The ambush will be here, Sergei. From the rise to the south." Vorashin nodded ahead. "Probably another hundred yards. They're waiting for us to move across those narrows."

"You saw them?" Saamaretz looked nervously at the hill. "I don't see anything." Behind him the tracked vehicles had already stopped.

"Shut up, Major," Vorashin snapped. To Sergei he said, "Drop the men into a perimeter I formation. I want two RPGs at the point. Have the Grails manned and ready. Instruct the missile team to arm four weapons with short-trajectory HE set for airburst to fire on my command." He glanced down the sled paths left by the point patrol's snowmobiles. "They've mined the area ahead. Fuel drums buried in the snow. Somewhere snipers are watching us very closely, I think."

He looked back at Devenko. "Do it quietly, Sergei. I don't want them to see a lot of running and yelling. Let them think we are being extra cautious. Yes?"

Devenko nodded. "What will be your signal, Colonel?"

"I will let the American commander commit first," Vorashin said with a slow smile. His expression changed again. "Target the crest of the hill. When you are ready, send my command vehicle ahead. All others will wait. Do it now, Sergei."

Without acknowledging, Devenko turned and walked to the command car. He barked at a wounded soldier who'd been riding on the running board to get back to his unit. He patted a platoon commander on the back and spoke to him rapidly, smiling all the while, as if he had a joke to tell. They strolled past the missile carrier and Devenko called up pleasantly to the launch commander.

Vorashin shook his head. "You are a wicked scoundrel, Sergei Ivanovich Devenko," he said to himself.

"Where are the Americans?" Saamaretz demanded urgently in a low voice. "How do you know they are here? I don't see anything. How *can* you know? Are you trying to impress me with some maneuver to—"

"I know they are here because they *are* here, Major."

Saamaretz looked toward the bumpy moguls ahead. "How do you know they have mined this area? What do you see?" His voice had that dry resonance of a man terribly frightened who was trying to suppress it. "How do you know they have buried fuel drums in the snow, Colonel? How could you possibly know that?"

"*Shallowly* buried," Vorashin said. "The tops are just below the surface."

"And you have eyes that can see this?"

"No."

"Then—"

"You would do best to return to the communications vehicle, Major," Vorashin said. "In a short time there

will be much shooting." He took his field glasses from
the case and scanned the frozen river to the north,
purposely directing his attention away from the hill.

"I want to know about the mines!" Saamaretz insisted. "I *demand* to be told! Where are they? How do
you *know* there are mines? *Tell me!*"

Vorashin continued to pan across the northern horizon. Behind him he heard the command vehicle shift
into a forward gear. A squad of soldiers moved past
him carrying a heavy machine gun. He lowered the
field glasses and squinted at the swirling snow above. "I
know, comrade Major," he said slowly, "because I am
standing on one." He glanced at the KGB man and
offered a grim smile. *"Now* will you move?"

Caffey was sweating inside his insulated parka. The
column had stopped dead at the edge of the choke
point. For two minutes it hadn't budged. There was
some activity but nothing to indicate that anyone was
overly suspicious. They were just taking special precau-
tions, he told himself. It was logical, he told himself. It
was the smart thing to do. But something in the pit of
his stomach didn't agree. They were almost *too* careful.

He held the binoculars on the figure out front, the
man obviously in charge. But his expression gave
nothing away—not worry, not concern, not even bore-
dom, nothing. Whoever he was, he was a cool sonofabitch.

When the lead vehicle began to move, Parsons
nudged an elbow into him.

"They're moving," he croaked hoarsely. Even Parsons sensed it, Caffey thought.

"Stand by on the flare," Caffey said. "When they're
in the middle . . ." He stopped when he realized that
only the first track was moving.

"Sir, just the—"

"I know, I know!" Caffey shot back. He focused on
the strike-force leader. "I don't like this," he said
softly. "I don't like this."

"What are they doing?" Parsons said.

"I wish the hell I knew."

Cordobes came running in a crouch below the crest. He slid to a stop at Caffey's feet. "Colonel, they're only moving one vehicle at a time!"

"Goddamnit, Captain, do you think I'm blind!"

"No, sir, I—"

"Get back to your position!"

"But what are we going to do?"

"I'll let you know! Now get back to your men!" Caffey swung the binoculars back to the column. The command vehicle was moving slowly into the choke point. A company of troops moved to the near flank. Someone started directing traffic—the other vehicles slid into rank formation, but they didn't enter the choke. Caffey found the strike-force leader again. He was walking toward the missile-launcher and glanced back over his shoulder at the hill. "He knows," Caffey whispered. "The bastard knows!" He slapped Parsons in the ribs. "Start the choppers!"

"Now?"

"We're getting the hell out of here!"

"But—"

"They *know* we're here, goddamnit! *Move!*"

"Yes, *sir!*" Parsons scooted backward on his belly, then jumped to his feet, breaking into a run halfway down the hill.

Caffey inched back from the crest and got on the radio. "This is Caffey to all sections," he said in a voice calmer than he felt. "I am aborting the raid. Repeat. I am aborting the raid. Evacuate your positions. Do it now." He crawled back to see the column. He held the walkie-talkie to his mouth. "Private Cable, you there?"

"Yes, sir, Colonel," came the delayed response.

"Stay put, Cable. I have some work for you."

"Work, sir?"

"On my signal, I want you to pick off those fuel drums as fast as you can."

"Can do, sir."

"When they're all gone, run like hell to a chopper. You're gonna be the next to the last man to get out of here. Got that?"

"Loud and clear, Colonel."

The Hueys started their engines at nearly the same instant. Caffey glanced around to see Parsons and Cordobes counting off the men as they scrambled out of their positions. "Remember the phosphorus grenades," he whispered. Then he unbuckled his cartridge belt and took the binocular strap from around his neck. When he started running, he thought, he didn't want anything to slow him up.

Caffey kept an eye on the column as he loaded a grenade into the launcher on his M-16. He had three shots. Don't try to be accurate, he told himself—that was Cable's job. Just add to the confusion. Stir up the snow. Then run like hell.

"Ready, Cable?"

"Ready, sir."

"The next time I talk to you, you'd better be on the chopper. Shoot!"

Caffey tossed the radio aside and aimed the rifle. He sighted for the missile-carrier. I hope to God this thing works, he thought.

Cable fired. The sharp report reached Caffey at the moment the fuel drum blew up. The blast shook the ground so violently that the trees lost their snow. The orange ball erupted into a flame that shot a hundred feet in the air and with it a ton of ice and snow. Caffey fired the grenade by involuntary reflex. He watched its flat arc fall short of the tracked vehicles and explode in a shower of snow. He grabbed another grenade, inserting it hurriedly on the launcher. Then the return fire began. It was, Caffey thought later, like being the only mallard in the sky for ten thousand trigger-happy duck hunters.

Pine trees and branches as thick as a man's arm were cut in two by the withering firepower that poured out of the column—small arms, 30 caliber, 50 caliber, everything they had seemed to be aimed straight at him.

Caffey tucked his head, pointed the rifle without aiming and fired. The next fuel drum explosion provided a lull in the firing. He glanced quickly over the crest to see a company of infantry taking offensive positions. The command vehicle was on its side in the middle of the choke point, less than ten yards away from an enormous smoking crater. The main body of the column was scattering in the debris of falling ice chunks like an angry army of white ants. Another explosion rocked running soldiers off their feet.

Caffey loaded his last grenade and waited for Cable's final shot. The private had to have radar vision to see through that frenzied white storm he'd created. Caffey could hear them shouting commands, but he could only barely make out the vehicles anymore. The last blast was nearest the column. Caffey realized that Cable had picked off the drums with the farthest first, so that the last explosion would have the most deadly effect. If that was his plan, it worked. The brilliant light of the fireball pierced the surrounding haze, highlighting figures, and seemed to engulf the closest vehicle as it blasted men and machines off the earth.

Caffey grabbed his radio as he tried to aim his rifle. "Get out of there, Cable! Go! Go!" He fired the last grenade and started running before he saw where it exploded. There was so much confusion it wouldn't matter anyway.

He was halfway down the hill when he heard the high-pitched whine over his head. He recognized it instantly and dove under cover of a fallen tree. Cable hadn't heard it or hadn't recognized it because he was still running when the missile exploded thirty feet above him.

Cable was dead long before his body stopped rolling at the bottom of the hill. The impact area sizzled where a thousand bits of metal burned into the snow.

"Airburst!" Caffey yelled. He was on his feet and running again, shouting at the nearest helicopter, waving it away. "Airburst! Get out! *Get out!*"

The second missile exploded thirty yards uphill and

Caffey was nearly knocked down by the red-hot shrapnel that glanced off a tree and hit him high on his left arm, ripping his parka from shoulder to elbow.

Cordobes in the first Huey got the message. Caffey saw him slap the pilot's helmet and point up. The overloaded gunship lifted off, lumbering toward the west, away from the hill, as Caffey staggered toward the other chopper. "Get out," Caffey yelled. Parsons hopped out of the doorway and literally threw Caffey into the helicopter.

"Phosphorus grenades!" Caffey was wildly pointing back at the column as the helicopter rose above the level of the hill. The helicopter wasn't protected against a missile's line-of-sight radar like it was at Shublik Ridge. They were easy prey for the short-range Grail missiles. "Drop the grenades!"

Parsons popped the pins of two grenades and tossed them out the open hatch as the receding battle-ground erupted with two tiny flashes of light.

The first Grail followed the brilliant heat of the burning phosphorus and exploded harmlessly a hundred feet below. The second Grail tried to adjust its turn against the steep angle of the falling grenade and broke apart in midair without exploding. The men cheered until several more flashes from the ground caught their attention and suddenly everyone who could get his hands on a grenade was tossing them out the hatch.

Caffey glanced out the other hatch to see Cordobes's Huey. It was half a mile away and about five hundred feet higher. Caffey squinted at it, unbelieving. Nobody was dropping grenades. "Jesus Christ!" He reached for the pilot, yelling, pointing at the sister craft. "Tell that sonofa—"

A Grail drove straight up the Huey's tailpipe before Caffey could finish the sentence. He watched the explosion rip the helicopter into two major pieces. There wasn't any fire, just the flash, and the only sound was a muffled boom in the whistling wind. The helicopter just stopped flying, separated into fragments and

dumped Cordobes and fourteen screaming men into
the frigid air twelve hundred feet above the frozen
tundra.

"Sweet Jesus God!" somebody gasped.

Caffey only saw the loss of fifteen men, an aircraft
and several thousand rounds of ammunition that he
couldn't afford to lose. God forgive him, he thought.

Vorashin watched the surviving helicopter until it
disappeared into the distant fog. He wondered briefly if
the American commander was aboard. It would be a
pity for a man with such courage to die ignominiously.
But whether he was alive or dead, the contest was over.
The column would move again but without fear of
another confrontation. They would reach their objective now. There would be no further interruptions so
long as the weather held. The Americans were beaten.
The small band of militia would not return again.

"Alex."

The Soviet task-force leader turned as his deputy
commander approached. "What is the damage, Sergei?"

"Two vehicles," Devenko said. "The command car
has suffered a broken axle and a weapons carrier has a
blown engine. Still, all the equipment may be transferred to the remaining vehicles. We can be moving
again in two or three hours."

"Casualties?"

"Six dead, fourteen wounded, three critical."

Vorashin nodded. He turned his back against the
wind and glanced toward the horizon where he had last
seen the helicopter.

"Do you think they will come back, Alex?"

"No."

"They still have one aircraft. They might—"

"I think he would not be so foolish, if he is alive,"
Vorashin said. He was still staring at the horizon. "A
good commander would not throw the lives of his men
away in a pointless gesture, and I think he is a good
commander. He is beaten. It is understood."

"I disagree."

Vorashin let out a disgusted sigh as he heard Major Saamaretz approach.

"We should send a small party on snowmobiles to wipe out the remaining force," said the KGB man as he stopped beside Devenko. "We must guarantee that no more time is wasted on costly delays, Colonel."

"I promise you," Vorashin said impatiently, "the Americans will not return."

"Are you now a magician, too, Colonel?"

"They have only one helicopter left, Major. They cannot mount an effective assault against us with only one helicopter and the few men it can carry. The Americans are finished. Let's leave them."

Saamaretz stepped closer to the colonel. "You *admire* them, don't you, Colonel."

"It is not unforgivable to respect a brave and tenacious foe, Major." Vorashin looked at him directly. "Intelligent courage is a quality worthy of admiration no matter from which side it is displayed. I don't expect you to understand it, Saamaretz. It was never taught to you."

"They are the *enemy*," Saamaretz said sharply. "We do not respect or admire an enemy of the Soviet people!"

Vorashin glanced at Devenko with a smile. "And they say there are no more Stalinists left."

"I *demand* that you send a patrol to eliminate the enemy force!" Even beneath the goggles Vorashin could see that Saamaretz's face was flushed. "As political officer of this unit, it is my duty and my right to insure the safety of this task force!"

"*I* am the military commander of this column, Major!" Vorashin barked. "*I* will decide when and where we engage an enemy. The security of this special unit is *my* responsibility." He glanced quickly at Devenko, then back at Saamaretz. "However . . ." He nodded at the hill behind the KGB man. ". . . Since you are so *concerned* about the safety of our battalion, I will authorize forty volunteers to search and destroy the surviving Americans. . . ."

"That's better," Saamaretz smirked. "They—"

". . . under *your* command."

Saamaretz's eyes widened. *"My* command?"

Vorashin nodded. "It is your duty and your right, Major."

"But—"

The colonel turned to Devenko. "See to it, Sergei. Detail six snowmobiles to a detachment to be led by the major. I will expect them to join up with the main body no later than midday tomorrow."

Devenko smiled. "Yes, sir."

"You think I can't do it?" Saamaretz rasped. "That's what you think, isn't it? That I can't lead—"

"You will be accompanying men who know what *they're* doing," Vorashin said. "Try not to lead them too strictly. I'd like them back." He checked his watch. "Leave in twenty minutes."

"I will," Saamaretz hissed between his teeth. "I will!"

Vorashin watched him stomp toward the communications vehicle. He shook his head. "I am sorry to inflict him even on volunteers, Sergei," he said.

"Maybe they will return without him."

"I doubt it." Vorashin looked up the hill. "I think men like Saamaretz were placed here so the rest of us would not be surprised when we meet the devil." He pointed to the wind-swirled smoke rising against the faint horizon. "In a little while, Sergei, send a patrol out. I want their dead buried. We should not leave their bodies for the wolves."

Devenko nodded. "I will see to it. Does it bother you, Alex, about the American commander? That we are sending Saamaretz to finish him?"

For several seconds Vorashin said nothing, then: "What bothers me, my friend, is that Saamaretz was right."

# THE WHITE HOUSE 1300 HRS

General Phillip Olafson walked briskly into the Oval Office. He greeted the president and nodded at Jules Farber. He preferred to stand rather than sit.

"Well, Phil," McKenna said, "what's the Joint Chiefs' verdict?"

"We don't think you should leave the capital, Mr. President," the Air Force general said heavily. "Whatever the Soviets are up to, this isn't the time for the commander in chief to be away from center. And Iceland?" Olafson shook his head. "That North Atlantic area is jammed with Soviet submarines."

"*We* don't have submarines in the North Atlantic?"

"Of course, but—"

"Are you saying I wouldn't be safe in Iceland? It is still ours, isn't it? I mean politically. It is a charter member of NATO, isn't it?"

"Yes, sir, but Iceland doesn't have an army, navy or air force."

"General, if I were to get into any trouble in Iceland,

do you really think an Icelandic army, navy or air force would be of much use?" The president got up from his chair. "Anyway, the way I read this situation, Gorny is taking all the risks. He asked for this clandestine meeting. He chose Reykjavik. If he had any idea of trying something funny, do you really think he'd go to such trouble?"

"That's why we're very suspicious, Mr. President. It doesn't make any sense, from the Soviet point of view."

McKenna breathed a heavy sigh. "Must there be a sinister side to everything, General?"

"In my job, sir . . . it's what you pay me for."

"Well, *my* first duty is as head of state, the political arena," McKenna said quickly. "It comes ahead of commander in chief of the military. That's why this is a republic and not a junta. When I can meet with another head of state, especially the chairman of the Soviet party, I'm ready to jump at the chance." He glanced at Farber. "I think Gorny realizes he's made a terrible mistake in Alaska. I think he wants to stave off any further confrontation before this crisis turns into madness."

Farber nodded. "Perhaps."

To Olafson the president said, "There is no hard evidence of Soviet mobilization, isn't that true, General?"

"Not for conventional war, no, sir."

"*Or* preparation for a nuclear first strike?"

"That kind of evidence only takes about thirty minutes, Mr. President." Olafson tried to hide his impatience by staring at the floor. "You asked for our advice, sir. We don't like the situation. We think you should decline the offer." He glanced up. "Anyway . . . if Gorny really wanted to make some gesture against confrontation, why doesn't he call back his goddamn troops?"

McKenna considered it. He paced several moments and wound up behind his desk before turning back to the spokesman of the JCS. "Maybe he's tried. Maybe he can't get through to them."

"If we can talk to Caffey, sir, they can talk to their people."

"I just don't think Gorny would try to arrange this meeting to cover a strike. The man is not insane." The president sat in his chair. "Jules, speak to me about time. How long would the trip take?"

"Four and a half going; five returning."

"And an hour with the chairman." McKenna glanced at his watch. "Home by bedtime. Can I travel light? I mean *light,* Jules?"

"Kissinger went to China for two weeks. There was a total news blackout."

"Dr. Kissinger was not president."

Farber half-smiled. "No?" He nodded. "Yes, Mr. President, you can travel light."

"Good." McKenna stood. "Then I'm going."

Olafson's eyes flickered. "Mr. President—"

McKenna held up a hand to him. "Jules, make the proper notification to Moscow. I want to be in the air by 3:00 P.M." He turned to the general. "Phil, I think this is too important to decline."

"It's your decision, Mr. President. If you must go, I have to respect that, but, sir, I think it is imperative that we activate a Defense Condition Three Code."

"DefCon Three?"

"Yes, sir."

"No, it would stir up too much suspicion . . . on both sides. I don't need the press jumping up and down wanting to know why we've put the entire military machine on alert. No, we already have this readiness-test business. You'll have to be content with that until I return. At this point Gorny is not a warrior. He's a businessman. Let's see what he has to offer before we start baring our teeth."

Olafson let out a long sigh.

"I know what you're thinking, Phil. But let's give

Gorny a chance. Sooner or later we're going to have to begin trusting each other before we incinerate this planet. I vote for sooner. Okay?"

Olafson nodded. "You're the boss, Mr. President. I . . . I hope you're right."

"So do I, General. So do I."

## EXECUTIVE OFFICE BUILDING 1530 HRS


Alan Tennant walked quickly into the front suite of his office, loosening his tie and wriggling out of his jacket. He spoke to his private secretary as he crossed to his office door. "Sara, I need a quick shave and a change of clothes. Call Congressman Stout and explain why I missed our luncheon date. Tell him whatever you like . . ."

"Sir—"

". . . Bring my gray suit. Tell Brad Reeves I want to see him right away."

"Mr. Tennant—"

"Whatever I have on for today, cancel . . . no, ah, fix me up at least two hours so that I can be alone with—"

"Mr. Secretary?"

Tennant stopped at his door. "Christ, Sara, what is it!"

She nodded toward his office. "Someone is waiting to see you, sir," she whispered. "He insisted—"

"Who!"

"Senator Weston."

"Oh . . ." He closed his eyes. *Shit!*

"Shall I—"

Tennant waved her off. "No." He took a breath and reached for the door. "Give me five minutes, Sara. *Five*. Then get me out of there."

"Yes, sir. I'm sorry, I—"

"I know," Tennant said. "The senator can be very insistent." He started through the door. "Remember, five minutes."

Weston was standing at the window. He turned when Tennant entered the room.

"Well, well," the secretary of defense said with a broad smile. "Milt, how are you? I didn't realize you were still in town. I thought with the recess you'd be back out West, glad-handing your constituents with holiday cheer like most everyone else."

"What've you been up to?" Weston said grimly.

Tennant frowned amiably. He realized he must look like he'd slept in his clothes; he hadn't changed them in almost two days. "Oh, do I look as bad as that?" He shrugged. "Well, I guess you know about the little Christmas readiness test we're putting on next week. I've been up to my neck in preparations." He felt the stubble on his face. "I guess I do look a bit haggard, eh?"

"You've been in the crisis room, haven't you?" Weston demanded.

"Crisis room?"

"Don't give me that, Alan. You haven't been to the Pentagon all week. I know."

"Now, Milt—"

"I want to know what's going on," Weston said. He walked to a chair and sat down. "I'm not leaving until I get some answers."

"I don't know what you mean." Tennant went to his desk. "We're just—"

"If I hear someone else tell me that readiness-test story again, I swear to you, Alan, I'll call a press conference and announce that the president is putting the military on alert without informing the appropriate congressional leadership."

"Milt!"

"I'm serious, Alan. I want some answers. You owe me. Tom McKenna kept you on as secretary of defense because I convinced him you were the most talented holdover from Thorpe's entire cabinet."

"I know that, but—"

"You're an authentic patriot, Alan. You balance love of country with concern for the people. You walk that elusive line between the generals and the politicians. I can't believe you'd be part of a coverup."

"Coverup!" Tennant exclaimed. "What are you talking about!"

"Dorothy Longworth has been to see me," Weston said. "She believes Tom is sitting on something very big. She's just looking for the slightest hint of conspiracy to break an exclusive story that the president and his military advisors are planning some reckless adventure."

"Dorothy Longworth is an ass. You know that. She has her own ax to grind with this Administration. Christ, she makes up half the rumors that circulate in this town! She's not a journalist, she's a manure spreader. If that bitch ever took the time to sit down she'd drown in the shit she's stirred up."

"I wouldn't be here if I relied on what Longworth had to say. Fortunately, I have other sources. They confirm what I suspect to be true—that there is a major crisis brewing and the president is keeping the lid on."

"What sources?" Tennant said.

"Personalities aren't the issue here. McKenna's boat is beginning to spring leaks. Not to the press, fortunately. But I know something is going on and, goddamnit, I want to know what the hell it is!"

Tennant shook his head. "If there were anything to tell you, Senator, it would have to come from the president."

"I've already been to see him."

"Then I can't elaborate on it any further." Tennant took a shallow breath. "The president trusts me, Milt. I've taken an oath."

"So have I . . . to the *people.*"

"Look—"

"I'm *trying* to help him!" Weston snapped. "If there *is* trouble, let me help. I'm not a fool, Alan. I do have some competence. If McKenna is facing a crisis that is so important he's afraid to share it with a political ally, what does he plan to do when Longworth and her cronies get onto it? He'll be politically dead, that's what. And the party with him. Or do you look forward to four years of Wes Nichols giving orders in the White House?"

"No, I . . . I . . ."

Weston leaned forward from his chair. "Alan, trust me. Please. Whatever it is, you know you can trust me."

Tennant tried not to look at him. He tried not to think that at this moment the president of the United States was *not* on his way to Camp David for a short holiday vacation. Exactly eleven people knew where he was actually going, and Alan Tennant wished he were not one of them.

"Alan?"

Tennant glanced up. He was staring at Senator Weston when the intercom buzzed.

"Mr. Secretary, do you remember that you have an appointment in the conference room? It's time, sir."

"Thank you, Sara," he said into the small plastic box. "Hold any calls for an hour, please."

"But, sir, you—"

"Yes, I know. Just hold everything until the senator leaves." He looked up at Weston. "Your word, Milt?"

"Of course."

Tennant hesitated a moment. He stared at his hands. Finally, he said, "The president, Jules Farber and Kenneth Quade left for Reykjavik, Iceland, forty minutes ago."

Weston gave him a bewildered look. "What?"

"He's meeting secretly with Soviet Party Chairman Dimitri Gorny."

*"What?"*

"It's a matter of some urgency."

"Jesus, Alan! Why? What's happened?"

Tennant shook his head. He almost laughed. "Because," the secretary of defense began softly, "there are Russian combat troops in Alaska."

Weston came out of his chair. "WHAT?"

"You'd better sit down, Senator," Tennant said. "There's more."

## JONES'S STRIP

The wind screamed outside as Caffey and Lieutenant Parsons walked among the men. Four pot-bellied stoves stationed at ten-foot intervals in the center aisle radiated only enough heat to keep the hangar from freezing. The wounded, covered with coarse brown blankets, lay on cots near the stoves. They were attended by haggard men with stubbled faces. Parkas and arctic underwear draped across makeshift wire clothes lines reeked of perspiration. More were splattered with blood than weren't. Some of the men slept on tarpaulins with their shoes for pillows between stacked rows of empty ammo crates (the fuel for the stoves), but most simply sat alone or in silent groups, cleaning their weapons or staring mindlessly at nothing, mesmerized by the inexhaustible sound of the raging wind.

Caffey knelt beside one of the cots where a soldier lay on his back, half his face covered with gauze so that only one eye was visible. His dog tags identified him as Pvt. William P. Toole. Caffey glanced at his buddy sitting against the edge of the cot. He was staring at the fire through the stove's grate door, fingering a used plastic syringe. There weren't any medics. "How is he, Private?"

"His ear's gone, sir," the private said. He didn't look up. "He's asleep now." The young soldier glanced up. "There isn't any more morphine, sir. He . . . he cries when he's awake."

"I'll find you some more," Caffey said. He looked up at Parsons. The lieutenant shook his head. "Give him Thorazine, then." Caffey patted the private's shoulder. "We'll get him out of here soon."

"Yes, sir." The soldier nodded by rote.

Caffey climbed to his feet. "How many are we, Lieutenant?"

"Fifty-two, Colonel . . . that's including the eleven wounded."

They walked to the end of the hangar in silence. At the door Caffey looked back. "Goddamn," he whispered in a choked voice.

"Do you want to say anything to them, sir?"

Caffey shook his head. He pulled the parka hood up. "I wouldn't know what else to say."

The wind whipped at the two figures as they fought their way across the runway to the cabin. They passed the cannibalized helicopter left over from the first raid. The tail rotor whistled above the storm, windmilling a shrill cacophony like the screams of a thousand demons, as the tie-downs strained to hold the machine to the tarmac. The ghost of Christmas past, Caffey thought bitterly, reminding him of his failures.

Kate was beside the radio operator as Caffey entered. "Anything?" he asked as he stomped his feet.

She shook her head.

"Keep at it."

"We *are*, Jake," she said wearily. "We are."

Caffey slung his parka in a chair and moved to the fireplace. "We're down to forty-one able bodies," he said. "That includes you, me and Parsons. We're out of morphine, compresses, bandages . . . Christ, we have people wrapped in fucking blankets and gut wounds held together with Band-Aids!"

"I know," Kate said softly.

"They *have* to get something through to us! *Anything!*"

"We're trying, Jake."

Caffey touched his forehead to the mantle as he stared into the fire. "Goddamn them," he said in a breath that was barely audible. "Goddamn them all."

"This storm can't last forever." Kate moved beside him. "We'll hear something soon. We have to."

"They can't take it," Caffey said. "Those boys can't do it again. *I* can't do it again. One helicopter and a bucket of fuel is not going to stop those bastards."

"You need rest, Jake. C'mon." She took his arm.

"It's the fucking cold," Caffey said as he allowed himself to be lead to the Joneses' bedroom. "It's the cold and the snow and . . . goddamnit! I should have known! I should have hit them earlier . . . from a defensible position! We could have taken out the fucking rockets!"

Kate made him lie down. There were tears in her eyes. "Go to sleep, Jake. I'll let you know if . . . when we get a call through. You have to rest."

"They could drop us *something*," Caffey mumbled. He rolled on his side, only half conscious. "We can't send boys . . . against missiles." He closed his eyes. "Tell . . . Cordobes . . . briefing at midnight. We have to . . . think . . . something. There's no morphine. Have . . . to have . . . morph . . ."

Exhaustion overcame him before he could finish another word. Kate draped a blanket over him and sat on the floor beside the bed. "Someone will come," she said softly to his back. "Goddamn them, Jake Caffey, they *have* to come." She touched his hair, smoothing the matted lumps. Then she closed her eyes and wept.

Milton Weston dialed the number from the study of his Washington residence. She'd written it down for him because it was an unlisted number.

The telephone rang only twice.

"Hello?"

"Miss Longworth, it's Milt Weston."

*"Senator,"* she said pleasantly. "What a surprise."

"I wanted to talk to you—"

"Why don't we meet somewhere, Senator," she said quickly.

"No, this won't take long. I called you at home because I knew you'd be alone."

"I hope that wasn't meant to be complimentary."

"I spoke to Alan Tennant earlier this evening," Weston said. "Alan and I go way back. He trusts me."

"So?"

"We had a long talk."

"Oh? And?"

"It isn't good news."

There was a pause. "Look, Senator, why don't we meet somewhere?"

"No, I don't think that would be wise."

"The . . . Christ! Wait a second, Senator. Let me get a pen."

Weston heard the phone bang against something. She was back in less than ten seconds. "Okay, Senator, I'm ready."

"I'm only calling you because I think it is the proper thing to do under the circumstances. I want you to understand that. I wouldn't otherwise make this call. But I think it's more important that you get all this straight."

"I understand exactly," she said eagerly. "You said it was bad news. I knew—"

"I said it wasn't good *news*. I meant that in a journalistic sense."

"Just tell me, Senator. I'll make the journalistic decisions. What did Tennant say? I just knew that bastard McKenna was sitting on a big mess . . ."

"There isn't any mess, Dorothy."

"What?"

"There isn't any crisis going on in the White House

or anywhere else except in that lurid imagination of yours."

"Wait a minute—"

"No crisis and no coverup. No nothing."

"That's impossible! My sources—"

"If you have any reliable sources, which I sincerely doubt, then they are mistaken. There's nothing going on. I don't know where you got this wild story of a crisis, unless it's something you and Wes Nichols hatched together, but I promise you that if you print any bullshit I will personally see that Nichols gets full credit for supplying it to you. By the time people stop laughing, your so-called candidate won't be allowed into his party's convention even to clean up cigarette butts."

"You're covering for him!" she screamed. "You sonofabitch! McKenna bought you off!"

"If you think so, print it. Print anything you like."

"You know I can't print anything without confirming it."

"Why would you start verifying stories now? It never stopped you before . . . having the facts."

"You bastard!"

Weston nodded to himself. "Yes, that's the Dorothy Longworth I know. The shrieking, hysterical shrew. Well, nighty-night, Dorothy. It was nice talking to you."

"Don't you hang up on me, Weston! Don't y—"

The senator set the receiver down gently. He leaned back and put his feet on his desk. Who'd have thought fucking that woman could be so much fun.

## REYKJAVIK, ICELAND

The only meeting place that the Secret Service could find on short notice that lent itself to both privacy and security was the gymnasium of a junior high school that had been closed for the Christmas holidays. Red and green streamers were still taped to the walls along with hand-painted cardboard signs welcoming ninth-graders to "The Last Dance of 1983."

The Soviets had already arrived when the president entered. There were four of them in the center of the basketball court—Gorny, of course, who was seated at a portable card table; a translator; Madame Nadia Kortner, minister of agriculture; and Aleksey Ruden-ski, minister of external affairs. All stood behind the chairman. Standing at the other end of the gym, behind the out-of-bounds line beyond the basket, were members of Gorny's personal bodyguard detail. They were as grim-faced as McKenna's Secret Service body-guards, who were likewise instructed to stay out of the playing field.

The footsteps of the president, Farber and Quade

echoed together as they walked to center court. Gorny
rose as they approached.

"Mr. President," Gorny said. He smiled and offered
his hand. "It is good to finally meet you." His English
was heavily accented but precisely spoken, as if he'd
rehearsed it several times.

McKenna took his hand. "Mr. Chairman, you look
well. It's difficult to believe you've just turned fifty-
seven."

Gorny chuckled. "Fifty-*six,* Mr. President. And
thank you for your telegram. I was very much moved."

"I'd like to present Dr. Farber," McKenna said. He
turned slightly to indicate his NSC advisor, who stood
with Quade a few feet behind and to the right. "Jules is
my assistant for national security. And Mr. Quade,
undersecretary of defense."

Gorny bowed his head in polite acknowledgment. "I
am pleased to introduce to you our minister of agriculture, Madame Kortner, and Colonel-General Aleksey
Rudenski, minister of external affairs." He gestured
toward the interpreter. "I hope it is not a great
infraction of our agreement, Mr. President, but I
included a translator in our group. It had escaped me,
but comrade Kortner does not speak English so well."

"It's all right." McKenna smiled at the squatty
woman dressed in a severe suit. "I'm not against
anything that might help us understand one another."

Gorny and McKenna sat down opposite each other at
the small table. Each of the attending seconds took a
step closer behind his respective leader.

"I'd like to begin this, Mr. Chairman," said the
president in a pleasant voice, "by asking you the
obvious question."

"Of course."

"What the hell are you doing on my land?"

"Reluctantly but firmly retaliating," Gorny said
calmly.

"Finally—an admission that the force is Soviet.
Ambassador Orlavski has not been so forthright. He
keeps insisting that you've lost a satellite."

"It is an ambassador's job to be devious. But we are here, I hope, to discuss issues. Matters of urgency. We bear great responsibility, you and I do, Mr. President."

"Exactly how is your military invasion of Alaska a retaliation," McKenna said. He spoke precisely so the interpreter would get every word. "Retaliatory against what?"

"Your grain embargo, of course. There *is* nothing else."

"It's our grain, Mr. Chairman." McKenna leaned slightly forward. "In a democracy we sell our products to whom we wish."

"Grain is food," Gorny said with the tiniest impatience, "but you use it as a weapon against us. Withholding food is as criminal as poisoning wells of water."

"Are you suggesting that we should have no control over our natural resources? That we *must* sell?"

"Isn't that your attitude toward OPEC oil? Hasn't it been your government's policy for fifteen years that any attempt to cut off your oil supply would be interpreted as an act of war? We are obliged to take that same policy in this instance."

"We have no such official policy," McKenna said.

"But you do have such an attitude." Gorny's eyes narrowed slightly. "Mr. President, not only have you declared an embargo on your grain shipments to my people, but you have also conspired with other imperialistic countries to shut off our grain imports from Canada . . . Argentina . . . Australia . . . from wherever you can."

"Chairman Gorny, when you invaded Afghanistan, when you sliced into Poland, when you made massive moves to undermine the Yugoslavian government, when you attempt to subvert the entire free world—did you think the United States would ignore it? Let me make this plain to you, Mr. Chairman: We will *not* accept aggression in the world as an alternative to free choice. Any means that works is a means we will use to express our displeasure!"

The president's words echoed in the large gymnasium. For several seconds afterward the place was silent. Gorny didn't blink. He didn't move until it was clear McKenna had finished.

"Mr. President, for almost forty years, our two nations have existed on the brink of untold horror. I think we are at the very edge of that brink now, our toes exposed to the void beyond."

"As long as it is only our toes," the president said. "You know, Dimitri—you don't mind if I call you Dimitri?"

"Not at all—Thomas." The chairman's mouth hinted at a smile.

"I presume life is just as precious to you as it is to me. Not simply our lives, but the lives of our families and friends . . . our people."

"We are in agreement on that issue, I think, Mr., er, Thomas."

"But at the same time, our countries have so rushed and stumbled down a path toward weapons superiority that it has become an obscenity. As rational men, you and I know that a nuclear exchange on any level would be a disaster of criminal proportions."

"I was hoping that the mention of war would not even be raised at this meeting," Gorny said.

McKenna looked at him in amazement. "No? Mr. Chairman, forgive me for being blunt, but neither of us came two thousand miles on a few hours' notice to sit at a rickety card table in a freezing high school gymnasium in the middle of Iceland to discuss the relative merits of arm wrestling. We came here because"—he took a breath—"because something went wrong."

A Secret Service agent dropped a cigarette lighter at the far fringe of the basketball court. The metal case clattered to the floor with a resounding echo. Immediately Soviet secret police moved a few paces into the visitor's court. Gorny shot a bull's glance in their direction, and they retreated back behind the neutral line.

Gorny looked at McKenna with a patient expression. He sighed.

"I realize, Mr. President, that the best players in the art of summitry do not easily admit confusion, but I do not understand the phrase 'something went wrong.'"

"I don't think that you are looking for a massive crisis," the president began. "I don't think you want a major confrontation with my country. I don't think that *suddenly* you felt that our embargo was illegal or an aggressive act, provoking your government to engage in a most destructive and bizarre adventure on our territory. I do not think, sir, that you have *just* discovered the major unrest and the continuing crisis facing your economy and social fabric."

"We cannot accept your embargo."

"So you intend to blackmail us by cutting off *our* own oil unless we resume the shipments of our grain?"

"No one owns the earth's oil, Mr. President, no matter where it is found. It is the same with food."

"I see. So the world's wealth becomes collective? At *your* convenience?"

"*Everything* is collective. That, Mr. President, is not a *theory* of expediency. We teach it in our classrooms. So do you."

McKenna glanced at the interpreter. He was sweating despite the cold, whispering at a hectic pace as he sat between Kortner and Rudenski. The woman seemed to be staring at something beneath the table, but Rudenski's eyes were intent on the president. The minister of external affairs displayed no mood. He sat rock still and his dark Russian eyes didn't flinch. They were eyes without a soul, McKenna thought.

The president looked back at Gorny. "Sir, when you made this enormous error of activating a self-serving theory of collective ownership to invade the United States—invade *is* the correct word here, Mr. Chairman—you burned down the classrooms. By this single act of aggression you've broken the code that's kept us at peace. We aren't Poland, sir. We will not accept a hostile force on our sovereign soil. And we will not try to repel you with rocks and sticks for breaking our rules."

"You left no rules to break. You cut off our grain— *and we need it.* That is, in and of itself, tantamount to an act of war, Mr. President. And by your *own* definition."

"We have stayed at peace," McKenna said with growing impatience, "because we very quietly and tactfully agreed that there were no villains . . . only values. We discarded righteous labels and opted for a corrupt peace—corrupt as hell—but *peace. That* is why I say, Mr. Chairman, that something went wrong."

Gorny gave the president a gracious smile. He nodded at Rudenski, who reached for a briefcase at his feet. "Then let us try to correct any misunderstanding," the chairman said. He pushed three pages of a document across the table. "I've made it as simple as possible, Mr. President. No more than eight paragraphs."

McKenna took the pages. He handed the two copies over his shoulder to Farber without looking up as he read his page.

"Its very brevity will startle the world," Gorny said. "Imagine, when bureaucrats from every government on earth see this, they will babble with horror. Not over the content, but the concise language."

The president continued to peruse the document before him. "I'm babbling, too. Not over the concise language"—he glanced up—"but at the *content.*" He held the page up. *"This* is what you call correcting misunderstandings? Eight paragraphs that state your invasion is *legal,* our boycott is *illegal,* and you simply want a public announcement to that effect? Chairman Gorny, I don't know if you're familiar with all our American idioms, but 'fat chance' seems to be the proper response here."

The interpreter hesitated in midsentence. He glanced at McKenna with a puzzled look.

"Not fucking likely," the president said, enunciating every syllable with clarity.

The interpreter's face paled. He swallowed, glancing at the chairman. Gorny looked solemnly at Rudenski. *"Nyet,"* he said.

The KGB chief cocked his head. Without taking his eyes off McKenna he made a rapid response in Russian. Gorny nodded sadly. For the briefest instant, McKenna had the sudden feeling that he was talking to the wrong man. He had a frightening impression that Rudenski was in charge.

"Mr. President," Gorny said softly. "Colonel-General Rudenski reminds me that our special unit will be at the pipeline in under fourteen hours."

"I don't think they'll make it," the president snapped.

"Then, if not, we have no leverage. You have no problem. But"—his eyes found McKenna's—"how did you say it . . . fat chance?"

"I think you have totally miscalculated the American people," McKenna retorted.

"I am only concerned with the American leadership."

The president shook his head. "Big mistake. Whatever you have been taught, whatever you have heard, the American people, sooner or later, *are* their own leaders."

"Then it is to their best interest not to push the *Soviet* people further into desperation. Grain is less expensive than lives, I think."

"If that's a threat—"

"Please, Mr. President." Gorny leaned back in his seat. "I have no desire to break off our talk, but I do not know how much more productive continuing this discussion can be if you insist on rejecting our offer out of hand."

"Shall we at least agree to consider or *reconsider* our positions?"

The chairman smiled. "Meaning you'd like *me* to reconsider?"

"Of course. Besides, you knew I wasn't going to swallow"—he nodded at the document—"that."

Gorny didn't answer. He glanced at Rudenski.

"Wouldn't you feel much better," McKenna said, "if you could inform your Central Committee that the American president is being very steady in this explosive affair?"

"Yes," Gorny said flatly. "I'd feel better."

"Then it's done. The issue is frozen for, say, twelve hours. But *no longer*—we will not accept a *fait accompli* on our territory. You instruct your column to stop and I'll guarantee no gunplay. Fair?"

Gorny glanced quickly at Rudenski. The external affairs minister made no acknowledgment. Gorny licked his lower lip. "I will be in touch with you as soon as I have contacted the field commander, Mr. President," he said. "It is best not to make promises until all concerned have been properly instructed."

"But you *will* call me immediately?"

Gorny nodded. "Of course."

"Good." The president let out a sigh. "I assume it's to your benefit as well as mine to keep this entire affair within the group that has been coping with it thus far?"

"You want me to help you keep news of this . . . situation away from the American public?"

"That would be very much in *your* interest, Mr. Chairman. The American public does not know you to be an intelligent and rational man as I do. They are very stubborn and romantic about their country. And they might not understand this situation as well as you and I. They would see the contest in Alaska in a different light."

"Contest? Do you think it is a contest, Mr. President?"

"In a way, yes. But the people would see it differently. They don't like to lose."

"Then go home, Mr. President . . . see that *no one* loses."

"And you, Mr. Chairman, see that we have nothing *to* lose."

They rose together and shook hands, then turned and walked in separate directions to their respective entourages of bodyguards.

Within five minutes the basketball gymnasium was dark and empty with only the occasional loose windowpanes in the ceiling to rattle in the wind and echo softly between the walls.

## JONES'S STRIP

Three mortar rounds exploded on the runway at precisely 0200 hrs, disintegrating the moored helicopter in
half a second. Two more hit the hangar, splitting its
corrugated sheet-metal walls as if they were made from
cardboard, crashing them inward. Another explosion
caved in the roof of the Quonset hut beside the cabin.
The blasts' concussions collapsed Caffey's bed as he
was rolling out of it.

The clatter of machine-gun fire followed. A burst
blew out a window and killed the generator as Caffey
scrambled into the Joneses' living room. The lights
went out.

"They doubled back!" Caffey screamed. "The bastards doubled back!" He searched through broken glass
for his M-16 as picture frames danced on the wall and
crashed to the floor from the rain of bullets. Through
the shattered window he could see the hangar. It was
burning. "Parsons!"

"Here, Colonel!"

"Get on the talkie! Get the men out!" The room was

suddenly freezing. Shredded curtains flapped in protest as snow and wind shrieked into the cabin. The temperature dropped fifty degrees in ten seconds. Caffey found his parka. "Kate!"

"Here!"

He ran in a crouch to the radio bench. The operator was dead in his chair. Kate was huddled in the corner, under her parka. "Are you okay?"

"Yes, I—"

"Put that goddamn coat on!" He reached up and pulled the PRC-41 from the operator's desk. "Keep this out of harm's way . . . we lose the radio and we *are* dead."

"Colonel!" Parsons yelled. He had the door cracked and was on the floor with the walkie-talkie.

Caffey ran to him. Through the crack he could see the hangar blinking in bright relief. The night was suddenly filled with flares; tossed and tumbled by the whipping wind, their flickering brilliances cast the battleground with a grotesque kinetoscope effect. Like bumbling actors from a film clip of a Mack Sennett comedy, GIs danced hideously to death in apparent slow motion. The Russians cut them down individually and in groups as they came pouring out of the burning hangar.

Caffey grabbed Parsons by the arm and slung him down as the two-day-old lieutenant tried to run to his men.

*"Let me go!"* Parsons shouted. "Those are *my* men! They're slaughtering them!"

"Stay *down!*" Caffey shouted back.

Another mortar round collapsed the two remaining walls of the hangar. Then the flares burned out. One by one they burned out or dropped sizzling into the snow. Almost as quickly as it had been brilliantly light, it was dark again. The mortars stopped. The heavy weapons fire stopped. For the few seconds before they heard the screams of the dying, there was only the sound of the wind.

*"Now!"* Caffey said. He pushed the door open and

led the way. He ran south in a flanking movement to cut the raiding party off from the good helicopter, parked at the other end of the runway. That chopper was their only means of transportation out of this hellhole, Caffey knew. He had to get to it before they sent up more flares. There was a machine gun on it, besides. If he could work his way behind them with that gun . . .

Caffey was gasping for breath and searing his lungs in the frigid air as he made it to the Huey. Parsons and two other officers were on his heels. Without a word between them they loosened the gun from its swivel mount and lugged it and three tins of ammunition to a sandbag position. Then they waited.

The second round of flares didn't come. They waited twenty minutes, but there was no more shooting. No one launched another mortar. They waited until it was too cold to hold the trigger anymore.

The attack was over.

"Where did they go?" Parsons asked. "Why didn't they come in for the kill?"

Caffey shook his head. He stared into the darkness to the east. "I don't know," he said bitterly. "I don't fucking know . . . maybe we *are* dead."

# AIR FORCE ONE 2355 HRS

The jet engines droned through the darkness outside in melancholy harmony. The president of the United States woke from a light sleep, blinking rapidly until he'd oriented himself. He was alone in the main cabin, sitting at his place at the small conference table where he'd fallen asleep against the double-sealed plastic window. A Military Contingency Profile (MCP) lay open in his lap. His reading light was on.

McKenna had had one of those nightmares again. It was 1978 and he was outside Lydia's hospital room. He'd run from the governor's mansion, in his dream, all the way across the state. The doctor was the same doctor he'd known in every other dream because it was the same doctor in real life. The pained expression on his face never changed. Neither did the words. "I'm sorry, Governor. She's slipping away. All we can do is make your wife comfortable, and wait." She died in his arms, but that was the dream. Actually, she'd lingered on for another day and a half, connected to all the tubes and strobes that couldn't do anything but monitor the cancer's damage and report what everyone already knew was happening. He wasn't there at the end. Nobody was there, just the machines. That's why he had the nightmare, McKenna thought—to remind him of his guilt when he woke up. The dream was the fantasy, how he *wanted* it to be. You don't let something precious slip away from you without a fight, his subconscious seemed to be telling him. It wasn't like you were putting a pet to sleep. You should have been there. He should have, but he wasn't.

The president sat up. He set the MCP file on the table and rang for an aide. "Ask Dr. Farber to come in, please," he said softly.

The NSC advisor moved to the table sleepily. He had his glasses off, rubbing the lenses between folds in his handkerchief, and was unsuccessfully trying to suppress a yawn. He sat down wearily. "Mr. President." He held his watch toward the light of the reading lamp. "Home in less than two hours."

"I've been reading that again, Jules," McKenna said, nodding at the MCP folder. "I've been thinking about our entire position with the Soviets."

Farber placed the glasses over his face. "Yes?"

"I don't want to be in a position where we allow this situation to slip away from us."

Farber nodded. "I see," he said quietly.

"When we land, Jules, I want to call an immediate DefCon Three. I don't think we can do any less. Do you?"

"You don't trust Chairman Gorny to keep his word?"

"I have my doubts about the chairman calling the shots, Jules." McKenna absently drummed his fingers on the edge of the table. "Gorny is a pragmatist. He's ruthless, but not a fanatic. They call him The Bull, you know. But Dimitri Gorny is success-oriented. In an American high-school graduating class he'd be the one chosen Most Likely to Succeed. He owns a big chunk of life. I don't think he wants to gamble with it . . . and I don't think *he* would even consider a confrontation with the remotest possibility that it could lead to war."

"That's the way I read him, too. But—"

"Did you notice, Jules—there were times during our meeting when he seemed more interested in Rudenski's reactions than mine?"

"Nervousness?"

"We were *all* nervous," the president said quickly. "No, it was something else . . . as if he were searching for some—I don't know, acknowledgment, I guess."

"You think Gorny is on the skids, that the KGB is running the show?"

"I don't know, Jules. But I don't want to find out the hard way. We just celebrated Pearl Harbor Day—I don't understand how we could *celebrate* it—but I'm not going to be the president that permits it to happen again."

"A Defense Condition Three is a first step, Mr. President."

"The Soviets already took their first step."

"They're not going to like it."

"I don't care if they *like* it. They'll understand it. They'll know it's a *defensive* first step. Hell, they probably expect it. The point is, we can step down from a DefCon Three at any time."

"Or a Two."

"Or One." McKenna made a face. "I'm not giving up, Jules. I have every intention of kicking them the hell out of Alaska before . . ."

"It's a hell of a game, isn't it, sir?"

"Christ, they're pushing when they should be thinking! Doesn't anyone in the goddamn Kremlin make rational judgments?"

"Wars do not start profoundly, Mr. President. They generally begin with cheap shots or ridiculous accidents."

"We will *not* be shoved into war. I will *not* be the

American president who historians say was responsible for nuclear genocide."

"If there are any historians left, Mr. President, they will do an autopsy on our species . . . to see what makes us smarter than turnips"—Farber shrugged, reaching for his handkerchief—"if we are."

## MOSCOW

Gorny squinted as the next slide filled the projection screen. He was not in a mood to watch satellite photos at this hour of the morning. He'd only been back from Iceland for a few hours when he received Rudenski's urgent call to come quickly—the Americans were making military preparations. So he came. He sat in the special Kremlin projection room with Rudenski and Marshal of the Soviet Armies Victor Budner and a handful of other generals from Moscow Center while a colonel with a remote-control button sat mutely to one side and commanded the slides onto the screen with his thumb while Budner and Rudenski provided the narrative. Gorny didn't like being here. He didn't need slides. He preferred photos. And, besides, this was the coldest room in the Kremlin.

"These are only two hours old, comrade Chairman," Marshal Budner was saying. "US Minutemen silos. You see, they have taken crisis-alert configurations."

Another slide flashed on the screen.

"Notice that our reconnaissance photos reveal security lockups of the missile bases. Undoubtedly they are beginning to seal off underground bunkers."

Another slide, this time an air base.

"And here, B-52s on alert, Seventh Bomb Wing, Carswell, Texas . . . Forty-second Bomb Wing, Loring, Maine . . . Second Bomb Wing, Bossier City, Louisiana . . ."

"Forty-five minutes ago," Rudenski said, "the aircraft carrier *Eisenhower* left Subic Bay. Its departure was *unscheduled*."

"And here, comrade Chairman—"

"Enough!" Gorny exclaimed. "Turn off that damn machine, Colonel, and put on the lights." The overhead lights flickered on and the chairman looked away from the brightness.

"The Americans have instituted a DefCon Three," Budner said dramatically.

"Of course they have," Gorny snapped. "What did you expect?" He looked at Rudenski. "And *they* know that *we* know they have."

"The first-stage alert is purely cosmetic," Rudenski said.

"Nothing from this point will be cosmetic, General Rudenski. President McKenna is a spirited man. He has a keen sense for his people. I would not want to press him too far."

"He isn't part of their military clique," Rudenski countered. "He has no stomach for war, comrade."

Gorny's eyes narrowed. "And we do?"

"The Americans will not go to war over grain. They would *never* institute a first strike under any circumstances." Rudenski spoke as if he were reading it. "The DefCon Three is for us to see, not for them to use."

"Any issue of first strike has already been established as far as the Americans are concerned," Gorny said. "*We* have combat troops in *their* country. Any action that they take while *that* circumstance continues is logically, and *legally,* defensive."

Rudenski nodded patiently. "Yes, it is a move, I agree, but just a move. They're compensating, comrade Chairman. They know as well as we do that a first strike on their part could only trigger our greatly superior second-strike capabilities. The Americans know how to count warheads. We have taught them how to count, if nothing else. They know we can survive their first strike."

"Do they really?"

"Of course!" Rudenski very nearly shouted. "How many times must *you* be told that, comrade Chairman?"

"How many times? I'll tell you how many! A *million* times! That's how many times I have to be told we can survive a nuclear war . . . a million times!"

"But comrade Chairman," Marshal Budner began diplomatically, "on paper we can—"

"A billion pieces of paper cannot purge the uncountable dead that would result in a nuclear exchange! Why do you insist on being blind to the fact that war would destroy us! We would lose, comrades, as surely as we would be the ultimate victors! Do you *want* to live in a land populated by ghosts and rotting bodies?"

"It will never get to that point," Rudenski said. "I guarantee you, comrade. Now that I have met President McKenna, I'm more convinced than ever before. He would not allow a war. He will back down from us . . . and we will have our grain."

Gorny looked slowly around the room. "I think, comrade Rudenski, that we have not met the same man."

The colonel general strode to the front of the room and stood before the projection screen. "If the Americans want to play games, so let it be. They've ordered a DefCon Three . . . we'll counter with a Mach Eagle."

Budner nodded. "Mach Eagle is amiable enough."

"Amiable?" Gorny's eyes grew wide. *"Mach Eagle!"*

"As amiable as their DefCon Three. *And,* comrade Chairman, just as visible to them."

Gorny shook his head violently. "No!" He stood up. "I will not allow further escalation! This is madness, comrades. Do you hear me?—madness!"

Rudenski let out a long, patient sigh. He glanced at Marshal Budner and nodded. "Yes, I think Mach Eagle is proper. Also, I think your suggestion about the Arabian Sea is worthwhile. See to them both, will you, Marshal?" He looked back at Chairman Gorny. "Thank you, comrade," Rudenski said in a dismissing tone.

Gorny watched as the others began to leave. They'd already made their choice, he realized. He looked at Rudenski, his dark suit silhouetted against the stark white of the projection screen. "Comrade *Chairman,* if you please," Gorny said softly.

Rudenski only smiled.

## WHCR 0820 HRS

McKenna had gotten barely five hours' sleep before he'd taken the slow elevator ride to the subbasement. In eighteen months as president he'd been to see the Crisis Room exactly once, when he'd taken a tour of the place. But that was before last Sunday. In the last few days it seemed as if he lived down here.

This morning he was sitting in his usual place with what were becoming very familiar faces. They'd all gone home or wherever those people went since he'd seen them last, and they'd all changed clothes and presumably showered and had some sleep. The trouble was, McKenna thought, none of them looked very much refreshed.

Burt Tankersley had the floor at the moment. He was standing at the projection screen where a high-density black-and-white film was rolling without sound. The screen image went to a series of numbers counting backward from three as the film went through another splice.

"Also," the intelligence agency director was saying,

"our reconnaissance SS-71s have spotted their new aircraft carrier *Kiev*." He pointed to a ship which was obviously an aircraft carrier and the only vessel on the screen. "It had been stationed off Ocha in the Okhotsk Sea. At 5:00 A.M. Eastern Standard Time it changed course for the Bering Strait."

"And destroyers," Admiral Blanchard said. "Four of their heavy destroyers of the Krivak Class are on an interception course that would link up with the *Kiev* south of the Attu Island string in the Aleutians."

"What does that mean to me in terms I can understand," McKenna said with a sigh.

"They are basically ASW destroyers, Mr. President," the admiral said as if he hadn't heard, "with E2 Class cruise missiles and SSN3 nuclear warheads. Those missiles have an effective range of eight hundred miles."

The screen flashed to shots of Soviet fighters.

"They're mobilizing all across Eastern Europe," Tankersley continued, "*and* their China border."

The president leaned forward slightly. "You mean they are mounting forces on *all* fronts?"

"That's Soviet SOP," General Olafson said. The Chairman of the Joint Chiefs of Staff clicked his pipe against his ashtray. "Wherever a confrontation flares up, they are flexible enough to start something ten thousand miles away. We do the same thing, of course, but our MO is strictly reactionary."

Tankersley nodded. "Our radio-monitoring satellites also show a radical increase in their coded and scrambled communications—up sixty-eight percent in the last six hours. We interpret that to mean the Soviets expect to do some heavy moving of material."

The president nodded. "I see." He waved at the screen. "That's enough show-and-tell, Burt. I think I get the picture here."

"They've gone to Mach Eagle, Mr. President," General Olafson said. "And they want *us* to know it."

"Well, now we know." He glanced at Farber. "I'm disappointed, Jules. Gorny agreed to hold off. I'm disappointed, but"—he shrugged—"I guess, not terribly surprised."

"I think we have to call them on this, Mr. President." It was Max Schriff for the army.

"Call them on it?" McKenna glanced down the table at the general. "What do you suggest, Max?"

"They went to Mach Eagle. I think we should bump *our* alert code up a notch, too."

"Bump, Max? This isn't a poker game. You mean go to Defense Condition Two?"

The telephone rang beside the president and Farber picked it up.

"Yes, sir," Schriff replied. "Strategically, it makes sense to keep one step ahead."

"No." McKenna shook his head. "There is plenty of time for the Soviets to pull back. Anyway, what they're doing is only a preparatory first step. The same thing we've done. I'm not in the mood to start World War Three, gentlemen." He sent an accusing glance down the table to Schriff. "I don't want to start 'bumping' for no apparent reason . . . we could all wake up in hell." The president looked at Farber, who was writing furiously on his pad and talking rapidly into the mouthpiece in a low monotone. "Jules?"

Farber held up his hand with a wait-a-second-I'm-busy glance. He scribbled some more while the president and everyone else waited. The national security advisor depressed the hold button and a small light blinked on below the unmarked dial.

"What's the matter, Jules? You look like they just shot your favorite horse." McKenna smiled at his try at humor, but Farber didn't acknowledge it.

"It's TAC COM," Farber said solemnly. "They've finally reestablished communications with Colonel Caffey's command."

"Good, I—"

"Caffey was hit last night, Mr. President," Farber interrupted. "The Soviets all but wiped him out."

"What?"

"He's on a patch through TAC COM. He's—" Farber

shrugged. "They say he's cursing everyone from Fairbanks to the Pentagon. They think he's a little hysterical. He's been asking, well . . . demanding to speak· to"—he glanced at his pad—"'the head fucking asshole.'"

McKenna made an angry face. "He isn't up there to *make* demands! He's up there to carry them out!" He reached for the phone.

Farber covered the receiver with his hand. "There's one more thing, Mr. President. It's from TAC COM's weather." His mouth hinted a smile. "It's the good news."

"Well?"

"The weather is breaking. They say that within the next twenty-four hours they can get air support to Caffey."

"Goddamn right!" Olafson said with a wide grin.

The president didn't smile. He looked at the large clock above the projection screen. "That may be comforting to you, Phil, but the Soviet's timetable calls for their people to be at White Hill in just under *ten* hours." He glanced at Farber. "Unless Caffey can pull another miracle."

Farber took his hand away from the phone. "Exactly, Mr. President."

McKenna nodded. He exhaled a heavy breath. "We're a handful of real sonofabitches, aren't we, Jules?" He picked up the receiver. "Hello," he said evenly, "this is the head fucking asshole speaking."


Caffey had moved his CP to the bedroom. The main room of the cabin had been patched up and was now a hospital ward which was crowded with wounded. Except he had nothing to give them. All the medical supplies had been used up or destroyed. He was treating gunshot wounds and burns with aspirins and iodine from the Joneses' medicine cabinet. There wasn't anything else.

He pressed the headphone closer to his ears when he heard the president's voice again. It wasn't the best connection. The signal wavered between poor and worse; but it was the best he could get, so he waited patiently each time the transmission faded. He glanced up at Kate and gave her a thumbs-up sign. The company's entire officer corps hovered around the radio—all four of them.

"Yes, Mr. President, I still hear you," Caffey said.

"What do you have left?" McKenna asked.

"I had ninety-two officers and men the last time we spoke," Caffey said, looking at a list of names on a clipboard. "This morning I have nine people who can stand up . . . sixteen wounded. The rest are dead."

There was a pause from Washington. "I'm sorry for what you've been through, Colonel. I know it's been hell. I appreciate what you've done for me and for the country."

"You said it would be a dirty job, sir."

"I won't forget it, Caffey. You can believe that."

"What I'd like, sir, is some idea when I can get my wounded out of here. You said that there was a possibility that the weather would break soon. We'd like to get out of here, sir."

"Yes, eh, I understand that, Colonel. Believe me, I do. I'm here with the Joint Chiefs of Staff and they each send you a heartfelt 'Well done.'"

"My men are *dying*," Caffey answered sharply. "I don't need thanks, Mr. President. I need help."

"Look, Caffey, I'm going to explain a situation to you that only a handful of people in the world are aware of. The Soviet Union has alerted its military to Mach Eagle readiness in response to our Defense Condition Three. . . ."

"*We've* gone to DefCon?" He glanced up at the faces around him.

"Just listen, please, Colonel. I've just returned from Iceland, where I met secretly with Chairman Gorny himself about this situation. I tried to bargain with him, but I have to assume I can't haggle that task force of his out of there in the time we have left before they reach

White Hill. Everyone is talking about avoiding war, but the situation keeps getting worse. We are very close to the edge, Colonel. Can you appreciate that? At this moment the Soviets are mobilizing. They're sending a carrier task force in the direction of the Bering Strait. We are sitting on a bomb here and that's no pun. Everything rests on whether or not that Soviet force reaches its objective. We need a few more hours, Caffey. If you can hold them up just that long—"

"*Hold* them!"

"—until the weather breaks, you'll have all the help you can use. I'll send the whole goddamn air force to you. But we need that time!"

Caffey wiped a hand across his face. "Mr. President, did you hear what I said? I have nine people here! *Nine!* How do you expect me—"

"I have two hundred million people here, Colonel."

"Jesus!" Caffey closed his eyes.

"You said you still have a helicopter. What about ammunition?"

Caffey shook his head. "We're down to—I don't know. Whatever it is, sir, it isn't much."

"Whatever it is, Colonel, it'll have to do!" The president paused. "Colonel Caffey, I'm sorry."

"Yes, sir. I know."

"Hit them as hard as you can. Even if you have to use the helicopter . . ." McKenna's voice trailed off.

"I'll do whatever I can, Mr. President." Caffey glanced at the grim faces around him. "Sir, when this is over, I . . ." He took a deep breath.

"Yes?"

"If you could notify our families . . . personally, I mean . . ."

There was a long pause from the Crisis Room. "Yes," the president said, "of course."

McKenna set the receiver back in its cradle. He stared at it for some time and during the silence no one spoke.

"I've never ordered a man to his death before," he said finally.

"Colonel Caffey is a professional soldier, Mr. President," General of the Army Schriff said. "He understands his responsibility."

"Does that make it any easier for us?" McKenna stared at the general.

"No, sir. It doesn't." Schriff bowed his head.

The telephone rang again. This time the president took it. "Yes?" He listened for several seconds. A muscle twitched in his jaw. He glanced at the empty screen, then turned to Farber. "Put up the map of the Near East." Into the phone he said, "Yes, go on." He studied the map, listening. "I see. What time was that?" He nodded. "No, don't give me coordinates, Major. Thank you. Thank you very much." He hung up the phone and looked grimly at Admiral Blanchard.

"They've rammed one of your destroyers in the Arabian Sea, Vern," the president said.

"What?"

McKenna made a fist. "The sonofa*bitches!*"

"Mr. President, where—"

McKenna got up and went to the map. "At seven this morning a Soviet light cruiser—ignoring warnings by flare, horn and radio—rammed the destroyer *Peary* . . . in international waters." He stabbed a finger at the screen. "Here."

"Rammed?" Farber said.

"The captain reported absolutely clear visibility. He reported that the cruiser made no response before, during or after the incident. He reported that he made two emergency course changes to avoid collision. That sounds pretty premeditated to me." He stared at the map. "First reports say at least twenty sailors killed outright."

"Mr. President—"

"Goddamn them!" McKenna said. "What is Gorny thinking! *What is he thinking!*" He turned back to the table. "He's pushing. If he thinks I'll stand for that, by God . . . Jules, do I have any choice?"

Farber was looking at the map. He shook his head.

McKenna rubbed his temples. "Christ damn them," he said in a low voice. He looked at Olafson. "Order a DefCon Two, Mr. Chairman."

The air force general picked up the phone immediately.

## PHILIP SMITH RANGE
## 18 MILES WEST OF WHITE HILL

The communications van wasn't a spacious place to begin with, but it was made smaller by the extra ammunition and dried-food crates from the vehicles they'd left behind. A faint scent of exhaust hung in the heavy air, and despite the monotonous drone of the heating units the van was cold. Colonel Vorashin sat mutely in a cramped space beside the radio operator, waiting for the transmission from Moscow which was already overdue. Major Saamaretz, flushed with triumph after returning from his successful attack on the Americans, made notes in his little book. He was an insipid little man, Saamaretz was, Vorashin thought as he watched him from three feet away. He wasn't imaginative or particularly bright, but he had a shrewdness about him that marked him for political service. The party was always looking for such men. The KGB was, apparently, a stepping-stone to some position on the Kremlin staff. Possibly, as an aide to Rudenski himself. They were all shrewd, insipid little men as far as Vorashin was concerned. And there seemed to be more and more of them.

"Beta Twelve to Bearcat . . . Beta Twelve to Bearcat. Acknowledge, please."

The radioman quickly fine-tuned a dial, then responded. "This is Bearcat, Beta Twelve. We are receiving you clearly."

It was the ironic truth, Vorashin thought with amusement. From the first day he'd begun training for this mission the radio gear was a source of trouble. The Soviet-made transceivers didn't work properly in the subzero temperatures no matter what tubes or transistor parts they inserted into them. Then a special KGB technician came to replace all the high-band-frequency radios with new models. They'd been freshly painted and the dialheads restenciled. It had made Vorashin curious until he had a look inside. All the circuitry codes were written in Japanese.

"Colonel-General Rudenski wishes to speak with Colonel Vorashin," said a relatively clear voice from Moscow.

The radio operator glanced up, startled. Rudenski had never called himself. He handed his commander the microphone.

"This is Colonel Vorashin."

There was a brief delay, then: "Hello, Colonel. This is comrade Rudenski. You are well, I trust?"

"Yes, sir. Well enough."

"What are your coordinates this morning?"

Vorashin looked at the marks on the small map before him. He announced them precisely.

"Good," Rudenski said. Vorashin detected a certain tenseness in his voice. "Colonel, Chairman Gorny is here with me. He wishes to speak to you. One moment."

Saamaretz put down his notebook in stunned surprise. "Chairman Gorny? Chairman Gorny is calling *us?*"

Vorashin was surprised as well, but he didn't show it.

In all his briefings he'd been told over and over again
not to anticipate any political acknowledgment of the
mission. If he and his men were captured, he was to
deny any official responsibility. He would admit nothing except that the mission involved a search for a
missing top-secret space capsule. At the time it seemed
that the mission was specifically designed without the
knowledge of political leaders as an expediency—so
they could say they knew nothing of the mission if it
went wrong. But with the last-minute revelation that it
was entirely a KGB operation, Vorashin had begun to
wonder who *was* ultimately responsible. A military
operation had to be approved at the highest political
level. The KGB—Rudenski in particular—didn't necessarily require political approval. Vorashin cast a dark
glance at Saamaretz. "He is calling me, Major."

"Congratulations, comrade Colonel," came the
voice Vorashin had heard a thousand times on the
television. "The best wishes of the Soviet people are
with you. And, of course, our personal gratitude."

Vorashin frowned. Our? Since when did comrade
Gorny share or even express his gratitude. He de-
pressed the transmit switch. "Thank you, comrade
Chairman."

"I have been told that you have met with some
unexpected resistance."

"Yes, sir."

"I am also to understand that they were a small, yet
tenacious force."

Vorashin wondered how he knew, then remembered
Saamaretz and his little book. "The opposing unit was
superbly led, comrade Chairman," he said cautiously.
"By an imaginative and fearless commander."

"But that problem is now behind you, yes?"

Vorashin glanced at Saamaretz. "Yes."

"Do your present coordinates project your arrival at
the objective on schedule?" The chairman's voice
communicated a slight urgency to the answer.

"Approximately, comrade Chairman. We have had

some delays, but we anticipate arrival in eight to twelve hours, depending upon weather and terrain."

"Do you *expect* any further delays, Colonel Vorashin?"

"None."

"Repeat that, please."

"No further delays," Vorashin said.

"There is some concern about the weather, I understand, Colonel. There is a growing possibility that it will clear in fifteen to twenty hours."

"By then, we will be at the pipeline."

"You're sure, Colonel?"

Vorashin shifted uneasily in his seat. "Yes, comrade Chairman." He hesitated. "Is there some . . . complication with the mission from the civilian side?" He'd almost asked if anything had gone wrong, which would have been a grave error. You don't ask your most powerful political leader if he'd made a mistake. It only occurred to him at this moment that maybe Gorny hadn't known about it until now.

"Actually, Colonel, the Americans are taking a much more severe stand regarding your mission than General . . . that is, than *any* of us had anticipated. I've met the American president and we are working diligently to resolve this situation. General Rudenski and I have every hope of avoiding war."

"War?" Vorashin glanced at Saamaretz. "Avoiding *war!*" He quickly depressed the switch. "Comrade Chairman, I was ordered to reach the pipeline and hold it until I received further instructions. There was no mention of the possibility of war during my briefings. Has the American government refused to negotiate the grain embargo?" Only silence followed his question. "Comrade Chairman?"

"Colonel Vorashin, we are pleased with your accomplishment thus far. You will be further instructed when you reach your objective." It was Rudenski who spoke.

"Comrade General, please clarify the political situation."

"You have your instructions, Colonel," Rudenski said tersely. "We will await your transmission from White Hill with eagerness."

"Please advise the state of negotiations," Vorashin said urgently.

The voice he heard next was the radio operator in Moscow, signing off.

Vorashin set the microphone back on its hook. He stared at the radio dumbfounded. "What's going on?" he said finally.

"I wouldn't worry," Saamaretz said smugly. "Your concern is strictly a military one. You are not a political theorist."

"They are speaking of war, Major," Vorashin said quietly. "Do you understand what that means? Do you have any idea?"

Saamaretz shook his head. "It is not for you to question, Colonel." He finished writing in his book. He closed it and looked at Vorashin. "Comrade Rudenski knows what he is doing. I have faith."

There was the explanation. It hit Vorashin with shuddering clarity. *Rudenski knows.* Not Chairman Gorny. Vorashin felt his hands tremble. He tasted the metallic flavor of fear on his tongue. The shrewd little men with notebooks were taking over. He imagined Gorny with his head in a noose and the external affairs minister smiling at the lever. He felt the sweat at the back of his neck.

Rudenski knows what he's doing.

Rudenski paced in front of the party chairman's desk. Gorny sat quietly in a seat beside the window. They were in the "official" office, the cold room with the larger-than-life furniture and furnishings. Rudenski had chosen to be here, of course, and Gorny had refused to humiliate himself further by sitting at the desk that he no longer owned.

"You sent Marshal Budner to Special Operations to make personally sure that the Americans have initiated a Defense Condition Two alert," Rudenski said impatiently. "You have that confirmation. So, tell me, comrade, what troubles you now?"

Even Rudenski had dropped the charade, Gorny thought. He no longer referred to him as chairman. "Everything troubles me, General." Gorny continued to stare outside. "I have accepted the puppet role because I thought somehow I could make a difference . . . that I could contain your recklessness, at least, direct it where it would not mean nuclear incineration. But now, I think, I can only look forward to the bullet in the back of the neck at some point when I am no longer a figurehead of further use to you and your . . . supporters." He glanced at Rudenski. "Soon, I expect."

Rudenski waved an impatient hand. "You are a romantic and dramatic fool, Dimitri. There is no danger to you. There is no danger with the Americans, except the threat of danger. Their escalation to DefCon Two is meant to be a scare tactic and only that."

"Then let me say that their tactic is successful. *I* am frightened."

"Yes, I know. That is your trouble. You do not act with decisiveness. You *used* to, comrade. But those days are over. The Americans have picked your once-ferocious teeth."

"Yes," Gorny said, "so here we are . . . we and the Americans. Standing together deep in darkness, waiting for a whimpered apology from the other that will not come."

"Enough!" Rudenski stomped his foot. "Comrade, the Americans will *not* go the full mile. Why will you not understand that? You have continually failed to understand just as Khrushchev failed during the Cuban crisis. The Americans will go to the edge, they will threaten and shout, but in the end they will back away. You have not studied them as I have. If you had you would realize that they are waiting desperately for our next move. They need a move from us to make them pull back. *Then* you will see . . . you'll see who blinks first."

Gorny smiled. "It is interesting, General, how you can reduce the fate of the two most powerful countries in the world to a simple children's foolish dare."

"They will not initiate a preemptive strike, that is all you must remember. We can safely increase the pressure."

"Safely? I think you forget what the word means."

"I suggest that we send ten squadrons of our new 28B Backfire Bombers toward the US Pacific coast. It would be a gesture they could hardly misinterpret."

Gorny agreed with a sad smile. "Hardly."

"You will contact President McKenna on the direct line in, say, six hours from now. The bombers will take off half an hour before the call. In that way the aircraft will not have been spotted on their radar." Rudenski began pacing again. "You will inform the president that the bombers are, in fact, airborne. You will tell him that we do not need the bombers to launch a first strike, but that they are only there as an illustration of our determination. You will speak of peace. You are a consummate advocate of peace, comrade. You have even convinced me. You have only to express your resolve that grain or oil is not worth a holocaust. I promise you, McKenna will accept our terms."

"*You* promise?"

Rudenski nodded confidently. "Of course. Even McKenna is not a fool."

Gorny almost laughed out loud. "No, you're right. Finally we agree totally, General Rudenski. *McKenna is not a fool.*"

## JONES'S STRIP

A light but bitter gust pulled at the wind sock as Caffey loaded the last box of ammunition onto the helicopter. He shoved it back under a canvas seat and made a quick inventory before shutting the hatch—a dozen M-16s, two machine guns, ammunition tins for three thousand rounds and half a box of grenades, frag and phosphorus. For the first time since taking over this command, he thought, he had probably more weapons and ammunition than he'd ever use. He slammed the hatch closed, then jogged back to the cabin. They were as ready as they were ever going to be.

Parsons was helping Kate pack the radio as Caffey entered the cabin. The warm air was laced with the smell of curious antiseptics—they were down to a can of first-aid spray for the badly wounded, sun tan lotion, a tube of Chap-Stik and a jar of Vaseline for the burned and rubbing alcohol as a disinfectant. Most of the wounded who were conscious lay on their cots with blank, senseless expressions, staring nowhere. Those who could walk acted as medics to their buddies. Three men had died in the last four hours. All sense of nightmare had evaporated; the grim tolerance of death and dying was the reality now. The bodies of the unattended dead lay uncovered where they'd died. A shortage of blankets for those yet alive was the higher concern. There was no dignity in death.

Caffey moved to the cluster of men around the chalk board where he'd drawn up their final battle plan. Someone had printed at the top CAFFEY'S LAST STAND, and under it, THE MAGNIFICENT NINE.

"Lieutenant Hendricks?"

"Sir?"

Caffey cast a glance over his shoulder. "Start up that crate of yours."

"Right-o, Colonel."

Caffey looked at Lieutenant Parsons. "The wind is falling off. They'll be moving fast now. The weather's breaking."

"Well, Colonel, *we're* ready," Parsons said. "Corporal Simms here will look after the wounded." He gripped the man's shoulder beside him. The corporal's left hand was badly burned and wrapped in strips from a pillowcase. "He's been checked out on the spare radio."

Caffey nodded. "Call Fairbanks every half hour or so, Corporal. They'll get an evacuation team in here as quick as they can."

"Yes, sir," Simms said. He glanced at the wounded men behind Caffey. "I know I can't, sir, but"—he swallowed and looked straight into Caffey's eyes—"I wish I could go with you. I'd like to be there when you hit the sonofabitches." He held out his good hand. "Good luck, sir."

Caffey shook it, then turned to Kate. "You still have a choice, Major."

"Major?" Kate looked at him with a puzzled stare. "I think we can drop the formalities now, Jake."

"You can stay here, Kate," Caffey said. "I'm giving you the choice. You don't *have* to do this."

"Yes, I do," she said. She held her head up and smiled. "Besides, I'm not exactly the Florence Nightingale type—*am* I."

"No, not exactly." He looked at the other faces a moment. The Huey's engine whined to life. "All right," he said firmly. "Let's go."

# THE WHITE HOUSE

The television screen went white with the flash of the explosion. The familiar mushroom formed as contrast and color returned to the screen. Mountains outlined in the background gave the explosion scale. It was at once terrifying and beautiful.

The president touched the VTR's remote pause button and the billowing cloud froze instantly. A pair of the Oval Office's window drapes had been drawn to keep glare off the console's screen. Farber turned toward the president with a questioning look.

"How many megatons, Jules?"

"This is a twenty-ton test."

"And the Hiroshima-Nagasaki bombs were what . . . eight?"

"Five."

"And the Russians tested a fifty-megaton bomb twenty years ago?" McKenna sighed. He tapped the pause button again to allow the tape to continue.

"A thermonuclear device such as this," said the

television narrator, "exploding on a clear day at ground level, would create a fireball one and a half miles in diameter. Temperatures at the core would reach twenty to thirty million degrees Fahrenheit—two hundred times the temperature on the surface of the sun. If it were targeted on a city the size of Boston, with the Hancock Building as ground zero, every structure in the downtown district—streets, cars, buses, even the underground water mains—would be vaporized in the first tenth of a second, leaving a crater several hundred feet deep . . ."

"I hope to Christ Gorny has seen a film like this," McKenna said.

". . . ten miles radius, the blast wave with 180-mile winds would tumble or severely damage buildings more than three stories tall. The established body of scientific thought believes that this planet could absorb an all-out thermonuclear war . . ."

Wayne Kimball stuck his head into the room. "Mr. President?"

". . . but that mankind, its inventor, would become extinct as a species and—"

The president switched off the machine. "Yes, Wayne."

"Better pick up line two, sir. General Olafson just got a hot-line request."

McKenna picked up. "Phil?"

"Mr. President, we just got a request from Moscow for a direct line hookup," Olafson said. He sounded slightly out of breath. "Chairman Gorny would like to speak to you at 1530 hours, our time."

McKenna checked his watch. "That's not for another five hours." He cupped the phone. "Gorny's decided he wants to talk," he said to Farber. "But not until three-thirty. What's he waiting for?"

Farber glanced up over his glasses. "Another proposition?"

"He can proposition me *now*, for chrissake!"

"If he's having trouble convincing his friends"—

Farber shrugged—"maybe he needs the time to do some old-fashioned arm-twisting. Whatever the reason is, I wouldn't turn it down."

"I don't intend to." The president spoke into the receiver. "Phil, that is a call I do not want to miss. I want you and all of the crisis-conference members present when I take it. We'll meet here, in this office, at three o'clock."

"Yes, sir."

McKenna replaced the receiver. He leaned back into his chair. "Maybe the old bird has come to his senses."

"And if he hasn't?"

The president held his head in his hands. "Pray for a miracle," he said. "Pray for Caffey to save our asses."

## WHITE HILL
## 1250 HRS

White Hill wasn't a hill at all.

It was on the back slope of one of the thousands of Philip Smith sweeps that connected ridges and tundra in the vast cordillera that was the Alaskan Brooks Range. White Hill might just as well have been called White Slope except that it didn't look like a slope either. The sweep was so long as to make the angle of its grade deceiving so that a man standing on it might swear he was on level ground when actually there was a twelve-degree inclination. But no one even considered calling it White Inclination.

They called it White Hill which, all things considered, wasn't any worse than calling the Little Big Horn a river.

The importance of White Hill to anyone who knew of it was that it was one of the booster pump stations along the 800-mile length of the pipeline to help maintain a constant 1180 psi of pressure of oil flow— manned by a rotating crew of five for half the year and self-maintaining during the heavy winter months. It had been a staging area for equipment and pipe during the pipeline's construction phase, chosen because the area was relatively unaffected by crosswinds that swept down from the ranges. Its location was accessible and not considered dangerous to skyhook helicopters that delivered heavy machinery and equipment to work crews. The pumping station consisted of half a dozen wood-frame buildings, a four-bay garage for vehicles and the booster pump house through which the pipe ran. The pump house was also the location of the emergency shut-down valve. It was, incidentally, from this assembly of buildings and, during construction, the machinery that supported it, that the pump station got its name. From a distance, after a snowfall, PS No. 3 *looked* like a snow-covered hill. But it wasn't called Snow Hill because PS No. 7, forty miles north of Fairbanks, had already been named that . . . and it *was* a hill.

Jake Caffey didn't give a damn what they called it. As far as he was concerned it was an intersection of coordinates on a very large map. But he'd never seen the pipeline and his first impression of it as the chopper made its way east, to find it, and then north, to follow it, was awe. It looked like an unending funeral procession—a frozen silver snake held above the ground by Tinkertoy pallbearers. Only the snake was a four-foot-diameter cast-metal pipe and the Tinkertoy supports were reinforced steel beams eight feet tall. The pipeline zigzagged across the rugged contours of the Alaskan frontier, dipping into the ground on one side of a river or stream and resurfacing on the other. A thirty-yard swath had been cut for it through densely wooded terrain.

When he saw White Hill from the air, Caffey knew exactly how he would defend it. The pump station was only approachable from north or south because it was in the middle of several hundred square miles of timberland. They weren't enormous trees; nothing that grew above the permafrost line in the Arctic Circle got enormous. There were just millions of them—spruce, pine, yellow cedar, hemlock, willows—more than a column of men in a hurry could hack their way through easily. Probably the trees weren't so formidable that they'd stop a heavy tank, but the Russians didn't have a heavy tank. All they had were two tracked, cold-weather vehicles. And the only way to approach White Hill was from the north or south—where the pipeline followed the fire break. The column's line of march would bring it a few miles south of the pump station where it would turn north into the break. They'd *have* to come that way.

For a change, Caffey thought, he finally had some advantages—total surprise, position, complementary terrain and a weapon he hadn't realized until he saw it . . . a million gallons of Alaskan crude oil.

**1410 HRS**

Caffey saw the first snowmobile top a slight rise about a mile and a half down the breaker. He passed the binoculars to Kate. "There's the point," he said in a whisper. "The main body can't be more than four or five minutes behind."

He'd selected the best vantage point from which to direct the assault—the pump house. It was the last building in the group of buildings on the site. It faced the south breaker, enabling an unobstructed view of the column's approach. He and Kate had taken a position at a window on the catwalk above the pipe where it extended out of the main pump rig and through the insulated wall of the building. The catwalk vibrated with each stroke of the pump regulator. It was like sitting inside a heart chamber.

Shu-thum-de-DA . . . shu-thum-de-DA . . . Eleven and a half times a minute.

The regulator's slow but methodically precise action gave the place an eerie sense of foreboding, Caffey thought. Just what he needed.

Caffey flicked his walkie-talkie to transmit. He

looked for Parsons's position even though he knew he couldn't see it. Parsons and PFC Merano manned one of the two machine guns in the thicket on the east side of the breaker a hundred and fifty yards away. The other was on the west side, offset so they wouldn't be shooting each other in the crossfire.

"Able, we just spotted the point," Caffey said. "They're about a mile and a quarter from your position."

The talkie squelched slightly as Parsons's voice came back. "Yeah, we can hear it. Snowmobile."

"Sit tight. Let the point through."

"Right."

Caffey searched the treeline across the breaker to the west. "Baker? You copy?"

"Yes, sir, Colonel. We wait for your signal."

"Good boy. Charlie?"

The pilot didn't respond immediately. "Charlie, here."

"No screwing around, Lieutenant. Fast, low and out. Hit your primary and go. I need you guys."

"We need us guys, too," came the reply. "Don't worry, sir, we'll kick their balls off."

Caffey set the talkie aside. He looked at Kate. "How about you?"

She gave a faint nod. "If you mean am I scared, Jake, you bet your ass I am. Right down to my wet little jockey shorts." She patted the muzzle of her M-16. "But I'm ready."

"Sorry you came?"

"And miss *this* show?" She shook her head. "Can you imagine what the ERA supporters could do with this bit of propaganda? First woman combatant? Christ, they'll probably make me head of the first all-woman regiment."

"Just don t be the first all-woman statistic," Caffey said. He glanced at her weapon. "And don't grip the damn thing so tight. Remember, short bursts. Pick your targets. When it starts I'm not going to have time to give you lessons."

"Don't worry about me," Kate snapped. "I *know* how to shoot an M-16. I took the course."

Caffey raised the binoculars. "Yeah, well, these aren't cardboard silhouettes, Kate. They shoot back . . . and they're pretty fucking good at it."

"I'll do my share."

"Good." Caffey squinted into the binoculars. "Because here they come." He held the talkie beside his mouth as he studied the distant movement in the breaker. "Able, Baker . . . the point should be passing you right about now. The main body is about eight hundred yards behind. The tracks are leading. The infantry is marching in four columns. Christ, they've even got their weapons shouldered. They're gonna walk straight into it."

"The point's passing me now," Parsons said. "I think the sonofabitch is whistling!"

"We'll give him a danse macabre to keep time to in a minute," Caffey said. "Stand by." He slid the radio into his jacket. "All right, Kate. Time to go. You know where I want you."

"West side of the pump house. Yeah, I know."

"And for chrissake, Kate, keep your head down." He touched her face. "Please?"

She took his hand and squeezed it, then turned and started down the iron ladder, the M-16 strapped across her back. "This is when the fair young maid turns to the hero," she called to him above the sound of the regulator, "as they are being led to the bottomless pit, and says, 'Whatever happens, you know that I will always love you.'" She hopped off the last rung and hit the floor with a dull echo. Kate looked up at him through the catwalks grating. "I have something to tell you that I might not have a chance to say later."

"What?" he said.

She smiled devilishly. "You're a prick, Jake Caffey. I hope that bitch Nancy *does* divorce you. You deserve worse."

Caffey nodded. Then she was gone.

He took up the binoculars and watched the column's steady advance along the breaker, into the choke point. What a goddamn place to fall in love, he thought.

Vorashin tromped along with his troops, Sergei Devenko at his side. He could see the snow-covered buildings another hundred yards ahead. They'd made it, and almost without a scratch. He glanced over his shoulder. The wind had died to almost nothing. The sun was struggling to get through the overcast. The storm was all but a memory. There would be no air strike now, he knew, even if it were a perfectly clear day. The Americans would not attempt to attack them with fighter bombers once they'd reached their objective, and a heavily reinforced infantry would serve no useful purpose. Destroying the task force would only mean the destruction of the pipeline as well. And the Americans would not allow that. That had been the plan. And it had worked. It meant the negotiations would begin in earnest now. It meant his people would not starve, because the Americans had no choice but to negotiate. It meant there would be no war.

Vorashin smiled to himself. It had been a long march. It had been four hard days of grueling weather, costly interruptions and occasional doubt, but it was over and the proof was before him—a deserted pipeline station that even the second most powerful nation in the world could not reach in time to defend. Now they would rest. The fighting was over. The Americans were beaten.

"What are you thinking, Alex?" Devenko asked cheerfully, walking beside him. "What you will say to the chairman when you report our mission accomplished?"

The Soviet colonel nodded with a smile. "That, too."

"It will be a welcome change," Devenko said. "To sleep under a roof again and eat hot, cooked food. I was growing tired of a lumpy tent floor and cold rations." He looked at his commander with a conspirator's grin. "I have also brought along a bottle of special vintage that I have been saving for just this occasion. Will you share it with me, Alex?"

Vorashin clasped his second-in-command on the back. He smiled broadly for the first time in weeks. "Tonight, Sergei, I will drink with you. I will have a bath and a shave and put on new socks and drink your vodka. I will give a toast to your wife and your two daughters. We will even drink to the Americans for the great shiploads of grain they will send us. And when we have finished your bottle, Sergei, we will drink *mine*."

Devenko laughed.

In a moment, Saamaretz had joined them—he seemed always to be just around the corner—and demanded to know what humor the major had stumbled on in the middle of this frozen desert.

"Nothing, Major Saamaretz," Devenko said, grinning from ear to ear. "Nothing at all."

The political officer eyed them both suspiciously. "I think it is not proper for officers to laugh in front of their men," Saamaretz said before turning away. He was miffed, Vorashin thought, that nobody talked to him, which was his own fault for letting everyone know he was KGB. Probably, he couldn't think of anything else when he said, "You do not see me laughing. *I* am a soldier of the people . . . and nothing amuses me." He stomped off, reaching, Vorashin was almost positive, for his little book.

Devenko burst into laughter. He clapped his gloved hands together and laughed so hard he nearly fell down. Vorashin was laughing, too, shaking his head, aware that the soldiers around him were smiling. It was just the release of tension he'd needed. He laughed without inhibition until tears came to his eyes.

Fifteen seconds later, the world exploded in his face.

Caffey knelt beside the window and watched as the point scout got off his snowmobile and glanced around, making a superficial check of the station. The soldier wasn't more than thirty feet away from the pump house. Caffey looked down the breaker. He had his finger over the transmit button.

"Wait . . ." he whispered into the talkie, ". . . wait . . ."

He'd picked out one of the steel beam pipeline supports as a reference point. When the first tracked vehicle passed that spot the column would be exactly in the center of the choke. He waited for that vehicle with sweat pouring down his face. The track seemed to be moving at a snail's pace. Twenty feet, fifteen . . . He flicked his glance at the scout when he thought he saw movement, but the soldier was only lighting a cigarette. He'd never finish it, Caffey thought. This time the choke point was perfect. This time it wouldn't go wrong. He looked back at the lead vehicle. Ten feet now. He sensed everyone's desperate concentration coiled with his own—Parsons's, the machine gunners', the pilot's, Kate's—it was like a stiffling weight on his chest that took his breath away. Five feet. The scout would die first, Caffey thought. Kate and the soldier at the other corner of the pump house, each dug into their own little holes, would have him in their sights. They had only to hear the word.

"Wait for it . . ." Caffey whispered again. He could only see the support now; his brain had focused on it and blurred everything else. Two feet. He saw the shadow of the track a foot away, inching closer. ". . . wahn . . . mmm-oore . . . phh-oot . . ." Shadow touched metal like a dark cloud over water and with it Caffey's voiced boomed.

"Now!" he screamed. *"NOW!"*

Mayhem erupted between the treelines like an exploding star. In an instant, forty men were cut down in a murderous crossfire like falling dominoes while seven hundred more dove for cover, scattering like a terrified herd of wild antelope.

The split second it took Vorashin to yell and throw himself to the hard-packed snow was time already wasted for Devenko. Vorashin rolled on his side to see

him still on his feet, still backpedaling a few paces from
the force of the impact to his chest. The surprise in
Sergei's eyes and the sudden shape of his mouth as he
glanced dumbstruck at the jagged and bloody holes in
his parka were exactly that of a man Vorashin had seen
accidentally electrocute himself—he couldn't believe it.
In the moment before his knees gave way, before he
toppled backward, his wide, startled eyes found
Vorashin. His mouth opened and his teeth were red.

"Ahl . . . leeks . . . ?"

He crumpled like a demolitioned building falling in
on itself.

Powdered arcs of geysered snow, ripping the ground
around him, finally delivered Vorashin off his ass.
"Return fire! Return fire! Second company, flank that
gun to the east!" He ran for the protection of one of the
pipeline's support structures. A burst of machine gun
fire twanged off the steel beams. A soldier running
beside him was hit in the neck and dropped without a
scream. The entire column was taking fire from three
positions with nowhere to hide. Whole platoons were
slaughtered before they could get to their feet to
advance. Men wallowed in the snow not knowing which
direction to fire, while others ran or crawled for the
protection of the vehicles.

"This way!" Vorashin screamed at a squad leader.
He pointed with his pistol at the machine gun in the
treeline to the west. "This way! Follow me! Follow
*me!*" Vorashin moved parallel to but away from the
machine gun, diving, rolling, running and yelling every
step of the way—making himself and the men who
followed as active and visible as possible. The one
cardinal rule a gunner was taught was to concentrate on
the main attack. Do not be distracted by flanking
maneuvers; that was the job of the machine gunner's
support, the riflemen and snipers. A machine gun was
too slow and too heavy a weapon to use like a rifle. Its
main purpose was to create havoc and inflict the most
damage against targets of opportunity. This gunner,
Vorashin realized, hadn't been taught properly. He was

too nervous or too stupid to know that by redirecting his aim at Vorashin's six or seven men he was allowing a hundred others to coordinate a massive barrage of firepower.

The gunner learned his mistake too late. The volume of fire and grenades that finally silenced the gun were as if an invisible scythe had chopped through the trees around it—almost nothing taller than ten inches remained standing. Vorashin found the machine gun position shrouded in shattered and splintered trees. Then he understood why they had fired at his little group. There were only two men.

When he turned back to the column he barely could believe his own eyes. Rising above the oil station's complex of buildings was a battered helicopter with Alaskan National Guard markings, the sound of its whipping rotor blades just reaching him. It was the same helicopter he'd seen limping away from the battlefield yesterday morning. The same helicopter Saamaretz so proudly claimed to have destroyed last night. But it wasn't destroyed. It was hurtling down the breaker, firing at his rocket carrier, blasting great holes in the snow with grenades. But that wasn't what caught the breath in his throat. The sight that widened his eyes was what he saw at the oil station's pump house.

A river of oil blackened the snow as it spewed out of a two-foot pipe from the pipeline's emergency bleed-off valve. The pressure was so powerful that the oil shot thirty feet before it touched the ground. Hundreds of gallons a second, Vorashin thought. It only took him a second to realize and then he was running, yelling for the men to run, for the tracks to move.

The oil slid down the south incline like a tide of black ink.

"Get out!" Vorashin screamed. He ran at an angle almost parallel to the treeline. "Get those vehicles out! Everyone, *get out of the way!*"

Three companies had already dug into place against the shooting from two isolated positions beside the pump station. The machine guns that had so devastated the column in the first minutes had both been quieted, and the only resistance besides the circling helicopter came from the clearing inside the pump station. They were pouring heavy machine-gun fire laced with tracer bullets and launching grenades into the compound, collapsing walls of buildings, blasting craters into the permafrosted ground. They fired oblivious to the danger sliding ever faster toward them.

But Vorashin knew.

He ran until he tripped over the body of one of his men. He suddenly knew that the American commander hadn't died yesterday in the crashed helicopter. Saamaretz hadn't done the job he was sent to do. He knew because no one else would have come this far against such odds for this final, suicidal showdown. He knew because the bastard was in that pump house. And he hadn't been beaten yet.

Vorashin also knew what three company commanders obviously didn't know. Unrefined oil was more than slick, sticky, gritty goo. It was still petroleum. And crude oil, even in these temperatures, burned very, very well.

"Able, Baker? Come in. Come in!" Caffey growled into the talkie. He dropped to the slab floor behind the cast-iron protection of the pump regulator. The pump house echoed with the pings of ricochets. A fragment had glanced off the side of his head at the corner of his right eyebrow and his sleeve was bloody where he'd wiped at the wound. He'd turned the bleed-off wheel to full-open about the time the counterattack began. Bullets ripped through the wooden structure as if it were only cardboard. The south wall looked like the back of a target range silhouette. Sections of the interior chalk and paper wallboard had been blasted loose and Caffey could see the splintered round holes the size of a man's finger in the outside wall. Chunks of pink fiberglass insulation and white chalk littered the floor around him. A grenade had blown the metal door completely off its hinges and through the shattered door frame Caffey could see into the breaker. Oil had surrounded the first vehicle and was closing in on the rocket-launcher as its driver tried desperately to escape in reverse.

"Able! Baker! Goddamnit, answer me!"

"I think they've had it," came a terse reply. It was the helicopter pilot. "But *we're* blasting the shit out of these monkeys, Colonel."

Caffey crawled to a spot where he could see the gunship. It had made one strafing pass and was about a mile away, turning for a second run. "Don't come back this way!" Caffey yelled at the aircraft. He pressed the talkie transmit button. "Lieutenant! For chrissake, follow orders! Circle east! *East!* Don't come back down the breaker! Strike laterally! They can't see you coming from the east!"

The Huey gunship seemed to hover indecisively a moment like a dragonfly deciding which lily pad to light on next. Its rotors whipped up a frenzy of loose snow as it just sat in the air.

"Do it!" Caffey yelled. "East!"

The chopper moved. Maybe the pilot didn't hear. Maybe he didn't want to hear because he began another strafing run, fast and low, barely off the ground. "Tallyho!" was the last thing Caffey heard from the pilot as the machine sped toward the column at an altitude approximately level with the top of the pipeline.

"*No!*" Caffey screamed.

If the helicopter fired a single round, Caffey didn't see it. Two hundred Soviet soldiers must have opened up on it as the Huey raced into range. The helicopter didn't even get close. The explosion disintegrated it in a shower of flame and twisted wreckage.

"Goddamn you!" Caffey pounded his fist on the floor. "God*damn* you!"

The back door of the pump house burst open. Caffey rolled frantically to his back, leveling the M-16 at the figure that rushed in. It was Parsons.

"Colonel!"

"Here!" Caffey wiped blood out of his eye. "Where's—"

"Dead," Parsons said. He ran to Caffey and scooted to his knees. "Merano, Green, Pitts . . . they're all dead." He'd been hit in the forearm, Caffey noticed. Blood oozed down over his glove. "I saw the chopper get it." He nodded at the door. "We'd better get out of here, Colonel. There's only three of us left."

Caffey glanced through the broken doorway toward the breaker. The oil was still spreading. Both vehicles were stuck in the stuff, their tracks churning in it. Soldiers were moving in all directions trying to get away from it. Caffey looked at Parsons. "We just have one more thing to do, Lieutenant." He withdrew a phosphorus grenade from his jacket and pulled himself up. "Help me shut off this bleeder-valve. The idea's to burn the sonofabitches, not blow up the goddamn station."

It took their combined strength and more than a minute's straining against the pipe's back pressure to turn the valve wheel a full revolution to the closed position. When it was done they ran to the rear door without looking back. Kate lay with her head down and her weapon pointed at the rocket launcher as Caffey and Parsons dove into the hole behind her. The side of the building above her position was chewed and scarred by a hundred bullet holes.

Caffey pulled the pin and held the safety spoon against the grenade in his tight grip. "Keep your faces covered after I throw this little mother," he said. "There's going to be a lot of heat and a lot of smoke and God knows what else."

Parsons nodded.

"Kate." Caffey nudged her. "Goddamn it, forget the sonofabitches and get down here!" But she didn't move. "Goddamn—Kate? *Major!*" He pulled her cartridge belt and she slid backwards into his arms. "Kate!" He rolled her on her side. A ribbon of dried blood streaked the side of her face from a wound above her hairline. The M-16 she was holding still had its original clip locked in it. She'd been killed in the first minute. "Oh, no," he said in a whisper. "Oh, shit . . . *no!*"

"You'd better throw that thing," Parsons urged beside him. "There's just two of us left . . . and I think they know it." He made a gesture toward the column. "They're coming, Colonel."

Caffey emptied the air from his lungs in a raging scream and threw the grenade with all his strength. The safety spoon sprang clear in the air, starting the chemical reaction that ignited the phosphorus. The grenade sailed in a long parabolic arc, trailing smoke through bright sunlight. The clouds had finally broken and let through great shafts of light. But the static scene lasted only as long as it took the grenade to return to earth.

The oil ignited with a rolling *phhump* as the brilliant grenade splatted in the black snow. A wall of fire shot up, spreading out from the spot like waves from a stone dropped in a pond. The sun disappeared as suddenly as it had come, blotted out by the plumes of black smoke. The fire raced across men and machines like a terrible scourge. A vehicle blew up like a Roman candle, its exploding reserves of ammunition streaking the holocaust with trails of red tracer bullets. Men ran blindly in the confusion, gasping for air.

And Caffey fired into them. He was impervious to the wound that seeped blood into his eye, to Parsons, to the smoke that billowed up and engulfed everything around him. He just fired into them, one clip after another, spraying everything in front of him until he didn't have anything left to shoot with and Parsons took the weapon away.

"I think that's enough, Colonel," he said grimly. "I think you proved your point."

Rudenski paced the floor behind Madame Kortner. All the appropriate officials were present—Prime Minister Temienko, Foreign Minister Venchikof, Madame Kortner, Marshal Budner, and, of course, Gorny. He sat beside Venchikof. The chair at the head of the table—Rudenski's place now—was vacant.

They were all waiting for Rudenski's aide, KGB Colonel Suloff, formerly Major Suloff, lately released from custody by Gorny's special police with all records of charges against him destroyed.

When he finally entered the room, Rudenski was nearly in a rage.

"Where have you been?" Rudenski bellowed. "We speak to the president in less than a quarter of an hour!"

Suloff set his briefcase at Rudenski's place at the table. "I am sorry, comrade General. The delay was unavoidable."

"What does Vorashin say? He *is* at the pipeline, isn't he?"

"We expect that he is, yes, sir."

Rudenski frowned. "You expect? Is he or isn't he? We must know, Colonel! What did he say?"

"Our last communication was incomplete," Suloff said. He glanced at Gorny. "Our last communication had the task force within sight of the objective, but"—he shook his head—"unaccountably, the transmission was cut off. We have tried to raise them again . . . we are still trying, comrade General, but so far we have not been successful. We think that the Americans are somehow jamming the radio frequency."

"And how long ago was this transmission?"

"Forty minutes."

"Then they are there," Rudenski said confidently. He turned to Gorny. "The Americans think they are being clever. This trick will not work. The task force has reached its objective, comrades."

Gorny got Suloff's attention by tapping a pencil. "When you say 'within sight of the objective,' what distance are we speaking of? A few hundred yards? A mile? Ten miles?"

Suloff didn't look at him directly. "Within sight means very close, comrade Chairman."

Gorny nodded. "Yes, of course," he said politely. "I'd forgotten that."

"It doesn't matter where they were forty minutes ago," Rudenski said angrily. "Only where they are now. And Colonel Vorashin's command *has* reached the pipeline station. There was nothing to stop them."

"Then why would the Americans interfere with the radio frequency now?" Gorny asked. "If they haven't done it before, why now?"

"It does not matter, comrade Gorny," Rudenski said. "When you speak to the president you may tell him that the station at White Hill is now under our control." He glanced at the other faces around the table. *"We* are convinced that the task force is there." He looked at Suloff. "And the Backfire bombers are airborne?"

"Yes, comrade General," the colonel said with a nod. "They left their bases five minutes ago."

"Good." Rudenski sat in his chair. "Soon, comrades, we will add a new page to the history books."

Gorny leaned toward him. "Just not the last page, eh, Aleksey," he whispered.

## THE WHITE HOUSE
## 1526 HRS

"Yes, I see," McKenna said into the phone. He glanced at the anxious faces around the Oval Office. The entire contingent from the Crisis Room was present plus Wayne Kimball, his administrative chief of staff. "You've been very helpful, Colonel. Thank you." The president replaced the phone and stared at it a few moments before looking up. "TAC COM reports that they've just talked to Fairbanks. And Fairbanks just spoke to a Corporal Simms at Caffey's command post. Caffey left this morning for White Hill. There hasn't been any radio contact with him or his command since one o'clock . . . that's one our time."

"That doesn't necessarily mean anything, Mr. President," Max Schriff from the army said.

"Colonel Caffey was instructed to call *before* two, General," McKenna said. "He hasn't called anyone."

"He may have lost his radio," Schriff added lamely.

"Yes," McKenna said. He glanced at the pad he'd made notes on. "Corporal Simms also relates that he heard an explosion. He says he stood outside and—oh, the weather has cleared, incidentally, for you who didn't know. Not that it makes much difference now." He sighed. "Corporal Simms says he stood outside and saw dense smoke on the horizon in the direction of White Hill. Apparently, the CP and the pipeline station are only twenty or thirty miles apart."

"Smoke?" Farber said. "What does that mean?"

"I don't know. *Nobody* knows . . . except Caffey, if he's still alive." The president rose to his feet. "I think we have to assume that the colonel and his men are . . . have been unsuccessful in their mission. General Olafson?"

The chairman of the Joint Chiefs of Staff nodded. "Yes, Mr. President, I think that would be a valid assumption."

"Then we can also assume that the Soviet attack force is now sitting on *our* pipeline, right? Anybody got any ideas on how to get them the hell off without starting World War Three?"

The telephone rang and Kimball went quickly to it. He nodded at General Olafson, who took the extension.

"I think, Mr. President," Farber said, "that we are going to have to negotiate them off."

"You mean give into them?"

"I mean negotiate, Mr. President. Now that they have the pipeline—that is, they can shut off the flow—they don't actually *have* anything but a pumping station. I think perhaps we should back off of this and consider exactly what has happened here. No, no, I don't mean give into their blackmail scheme. But I think something can be worked out. Suppose we let them have the pump station for several weeks."

"Jules—"

"Please, Mr. President, let me finish. Suppose we let them have it. It wouldn't be any worse than if there'd been an accident and we had to shut it down for several days or weeks. You might consider that alternative. Those soldiers can't live there indefinitely. I mean, if the army surrounded the place and just waited them out, they'd have to give in sooner or later. And that gives us time. We *can* negotiate this thing, Mr. President. I'm sure the Soviets want that."

McKenna considered it. "Perhaps, but—" He looked at Olafson. The general was just replacing the receiver. "Phil?"

The air force general stood up, addressing the president formally. "Mr. President, our IDT radar center is reporting several squadrons of Soviet aircraft leaving their security fields one hundred miles north of Yelizovo. They have climbed to sixty thousand feet."

McKenna stared at the general in disbelief. "What?"

"At their calculated speed and altitude," Olafson went on, "they can only be the new 28-D Backfire bombers."

"Going where?" the president asked.

"Coming, sir." Olafson glanced at the others in the room before looking at the president. "If they maintain their present course and speed it would put them over the Pacific Coast in about thirty-five minutes."

"My God!"

"I've put SAC on alert, Mr. President. Our B-52s are scrambling, that is, they're taking off all over the world, right now."

"Now?"

"Yes, sir."

Wayne Kimball moved beside the president. "The Moscow line is hot, Mr. President."

McKenna continued to stare at Olafson. Then he glanced at Kimball and frowned. "I'm sorry, Wayne, what?"

"The Moscow line. Chairman Gorny is waiting to speak to you."

McKenna walked to the gray phone that had no dial. A light blinked on it. He turned to Olafson. "How close can our B-52s get to the Soviet Union without actually violating their airspace?"

"Centimeters or inches?"

The president reached for the phone. "Do it."

## THE WHITE HOUSE
## 1530 HRS

"Good day, Mr. Chairman."

"Good day, Mr. President. I hope you have been well since last we met."

"Well enough to want some explanation about why you have several squadrons of bombers in the air."

"I understand, Mr. President, that they are engaged in a special maneuver—scheduled months ago, I'm told."

"Why is it with you people that everything is scheduled months ago? Look, Chairman Gorny, I want those planes turned around and turned around *now*."

"I'm afraid I am not in a position to make such judgments any longer, Mr. President. But I will forward your concern immediately to those who are."

"You're not in control anymore?"

"I can only speak for . . . my people, Mr. President. It is they who are in control. The Central Committee has considered at some length our talk in Iceland. We wish you to join with us in a joint declaration. Oh, incidentally, Mr. President, I am told to inform you that our special task force has reached its objective in Alaska."

"Go on, Mr. Chairman. I'm interested to hear about this *declaration.*"

"In the spirit of brotherhood, in the spirit of peace between our two great nations, you declare all embargoes on the Soviet Union suspended for twenty years. The United States, which has always believed that food is an international blessing and not a weapon of deprivation, will, as a gesture for all the world to see . . ."

"Excuse me, Mr. Chairman, but what declaration are *you* making?"

"That the United States will have an uninterrupted flow of oil."

"Surely, you're not guaranteeing our own oil to us!"

"The Central Committee believes this to be . . . fair, Mr. President."

"I don't know what it was your Central Committee discussed at such length, but that offer isn't any different from the original one. I expected some compromise, Mr. Chairman. What you've outlined is no more acceptable now than it was the first time you tried to palm it off on me."

"Then nothing has changed?"

"Something's changed, all right. Your Backfire bombers are a significant change, I would say."

"I think the bombers are not a problem, Mr. President, believe me."

"If you don't mind, Mr. Chairman, I see that a little differently. Particularly since you are not in charge of the situation at your end. I see it very differently, as a matter of fact, which is why I have authorized the Strategic Air Command to take certain necessary steps. But don't worry, they aren't a problem."

"You have alerted your B-52s?"

"Of course."

"It is a very antagonistic move, Mr. President."

"Antagonistic? You have invaded *my* country and to

take appropriate defensive measures is antagonistic? Look, Gorny, you get your people off my land. Withdraw the unit and I'm sure we can negotiate this matter sensibly. But don't push, Mr. Chairman. Don't threaten me. You won't solve anything, I can promise you that. The United States will not—*not*, Mr. Chairman—accept any terms or agree to any declaration while there are Soviet combat troops on its sovereign soil. I want to make that absolutely clear to you so you can explain it to your Central Committee. Do you understand, Mr. Chairman?"

"Mr. President, *I* understand you only too well. Peace is the only imperative in this entire nasty business. I will present your views without delay to the Central Committee. I am sure arrangements will be made to bring the unit back. I will take your word that there will be no attempt to exploit this as a Soviet disaster."

"You have my word."

"And when the weather clears, your air force will not eliminate the unit?"

"It has been clear for the past hour, Mr. Chairman. They're still in one piece. You have my assurance that they may withdraw peacefully. And you will guarantee that there will be no damage to the pipeline?"

"Of course. And your B-52s will return to their bases?"

"The moment I have evidence that the Backfires have changed course."

"Then it will be done, Mr. President. I hope we will have the opportunity to meet again . . . under more agreeable circumstances."

"Yes, I'd like that."

"Good day, Mr. President."

"Goodbye, Mr. Chairman."

McKenna replaced the special phone in its cradle. For several moments he said nothing. Then, without looking at anyone, he said, "I don't believe him. I think Gorny was promising rainbows. I think he was speaking

for himself, not for the 'Central Committee.' Rudenski
is running it, I'm convinced of that. I felt as if I could
hear him breathing down Gorny's neck." He glanced
up at Farber. "Jules, I think they're going to come in."

"And if you're wrong, Mr. President?"

McKenna stared at his hands. He remembered his
special nightmare—the hospital, the doctor's face, the
guilt after the fantasy. You should have been there. *You
should have been there.*

"Excuse me, Mr. President?"

McKenna looked up quickly. "No, ah, no. I . . ."

"The law says you must notify the Special Congressional Committee." It was Secretary of Defense Alan
Tennant, looking as if he might break down.

"We can't wait that long," General Olafson said.
"Congress is in recess. God knows how long it'd take to
find all of them. This is a national crisis, Mr. President.
You have absolute authority as commander in chief. No
one questions that."

The president glanced at Farber. The Oval Office
was absolutely still. For once his national security
advisor had no reply. "God forgive me," McKenna
whispered. He looked at Olafson . . . and nodded.


"How could you tell him that!" Rudenski said.

Gorny was the only one sitting at the conference
table now. In his old chair. Rudenski was pacing, as
usual. The rest of the committee stood about in pairs.
Nervousness, Gorny thought. They know what's coming and it terrifies them.

"You hadn't the authority to speak for them! You
cannot interfere!" Rudenski clasped his hands behind
his back and conferred with Suloff a moment.

"It does not matter," Gorny said, trying to catch the
inflection Rudenski had used. "I don't think McKenna
believed me anyway."

"I *know* you, comrade, and *I* didn't believe you,"
Rudenski said.

"He didn't believe that you would turn the bombers
back because I don't believe you will. He believes you

will go over the edge because I believe you will. It is difficult to lie, comrade General, when you know you cannot win whatever happens."

Rudenski stared at Gorny without expression. "I wouldn't have, you know," he said after a moment. "I really wouldn't have."

"The Americans will be slower, comrade General," Suloff said quickly. "The President must have Special Congressional Committee approval. That means we have at least a twenty-five-minute advantage."

"Twenty-five minutes," Gorny said mockingly. "All that time."

"Enough!" Rudenski bellowed. "You are not a part of this anymore, comrade. You will be silent!"

"I was *never* a part of this," he replied.

Suloff looked at Rudenski expectantly. "Comrade General?"

Rudenski looked at the others. "You all knew this day would come. How do you say?" No one spoke. The room was silent. Rudenski turned back to Suloff. "The first-strike initiative is ours," he said without a trace of emotion. "Do it quickly."

The echo of the colonel's footsteps did not leave the large room even as he retreated down the long corridor and to the next and the next after that.

## WHITE HILL
## 1553 HRS

The air was acrid with the scent of death. The ground was black and muddy where an hour ago it had been white and crisp. The trees smelled of smoke and petroleum, but in the bright afternoon sun there was not a cloud for miles.

Caffey sat on his haunches, almost mesmerized, waiting for the end to come. It was here already but just hadn't caught him yet, he thought. What Russians were left had gone into the trees. Sooner or later they'd be out. Not that it mattered how many of them there were. Two hundred or two thousand, he hadn't anything to fight them with . . . and he didn't feel like it anyway.

"Colonel? Colonel Caffey, you'd better take a look at this." Parsons nudged him with his foot. He'd been lying in the same spot where Kate had been. "Colonel?"

"How many are there, Lieutenant?"

"No, it's not that, Colonel. Look. They're walking out under a white flag."

Caffey stared up at Parsons.
"No, really, Colonel. Look!"

They'd stopped about forty feet from the pump house. Four officers. Caffey walked out to meet them. Parsons followed with his empty M-16 slung over his shoulder.

"I am Col. Alexander Mikhail Vorashin," Vorashin said in heavily accented English. "Commander of the 51st Arctic Combat Brigade of the Ninth Soviet Army."

Caffey nodded. "Colonel Jake Caffey, US Army. What's on your mind, Colonel?"

"I wish the fighting to stop, Colonel. It is a pointless exercise now, I think. I have lost three hundred and seventeen men today. I do not wish to lose any more. We have lost our radio"—Vorashin motioned to the smoldering ruins of his tracked vehicles—"and I cannot communicate with my command headquarters for further instructions."

"You want to surrender, Colonel?"

Vorashin's mouth hinted at a smile. "No, Colonel. I would like to go home."

Caffey considered it. He sighed. "So would I, Colonel." He extended a hand to the Russian and nodded. "So would I."

A brief glint of light reflected from an object high in the stratosphere. It was moving beyond sound, heading north, trailing an almost imperceptibly faint line in the sky. Then, fleetingly, another reflected glimmer, traveling in the opposite direction. But neither man noticed.